for my children and grandchildren,

and in loving memory of my father-in-law

# THE GHOST OF MORGAN GULCH

VICKIE L. GARDNER

# 1

## MORGAN GULCH

Kyle thumped his pencil on the old wooden school desk. He didn't care much for English class. What was he ever going to use English for as a field geologist? The bell rang—finally. The kids pushed their way out of the classroom, laughing and yelling, drowning out the teacher's plea to keep up with their studies over spring break.

"Yeah right," blurted out one student.

Impatient and anxious to get home, Kyle finally made his way to the hallway.

"What's the rush, Kyle," said a raspy voice from behind him. "In a hurry to go chase ghosts over spring break?"

"What are you talking about?" Kyle instantly regretted asking the question. Looking straight ahead, he walked down the hall to his locker, cringing at the snickering and ogling eyes.

"Haven't you heard?" the raspy voice continued. Tommy followed Kyle. "There's a ghost on your mountain—a crotchety old miner's ghost."

Kyle opened his locker. "Yeah right, Tommy," he said, wishing he could crawl inside and never come out. "There are no such things as ghosts."

Kyle slammed his locker shut. His face turned red, greatly contrasting his blond hair. He glanced back at Tommy, trying to decide whether to ignore him or to keep arguing with him. The choice was easy. Kyle didn't like confrontation, so he turned and walked away.

Kyle rolled his eyes. *A haunted mountain? Who was Tommy trying to kid?* He thought. It was difficult enough to be dragged from his home in the big city of Phoenix and start school in an out-of-the-way small Colorado mountain town; now Tommy's bullying made it even worse. Though it was starting to annoy him, Kyle figured Tommy only harassed the kids to make himself feel better. Kyle headed out the main door, down the old wooden steps, and made his way through the crowd of after school gossipers.

"Hey, bud," said an unfamiliar voice, followed by a slap on Kyle's shoulder. "I wouldn't give that kid a second thought. He's been a bully all his born days. It seems no one's taught him a lesson in manners—yet."

Kyle didn't respond.

"As obnoxious as he is, there might be some truth to that ghost stuff he talks about." The boy dribbled his basketball in a circle around Kyle.

"I'm Kyle Morgan. And you would be—?"

"So you're the new Morgan guy I've been hearing about. I'm Chris Henderson. I'm your mountain neighbor." Chris was about Kyle's height with a similar slender and athletic build. Chris stretched his arm up into the air, making a friendly high-five gesture. Kyle smiled as their hands slapped in the air. He hadn't felt this good since they moved here to Morgan Gulch.

Kyle had been popular at his school back home. He missed the high-fives in the hallway, the shy smiles from the cute girls, and the warm welcomes from the teachers.

"Glad to meet you," Kyle said, stealing the ball from Chris. "Are you saying there's some truth to what Tommy's saying?"

"Well, it depends on who you ask," said Chris. "The stories say that a miner, maybe even two miners, died on your mountain. Ever since then, there have been some strange sightings around the caves up there."

Kyle felt the blood drain from his face. He didn't really believe in ghosts, but the thought, even the rumor of ghosts being on the mountain, gave him chills.

"What part of this ghost story don't you believe?" he asked. "The ghost part?"

"The part about the ghost's gold," Chris said, stealing the ball back from Kyle.

"Gold?" Kyle asked. He loved treasure hunting. Kyle knew some of the mining history of the valley, and if there was gold on their mountain, finding it would mean a lot to his family. Most of Grandpa's cattle herd had died during the harsh winter. He didn't have enough cattle to sell to the cattle buyers, so his bills had piled up and he was about to lose the ranch. That was why Kyle and his family had to come to Morgan Gulch—to help Grandpa with the bills and the ranch. Finding the gold could mean paying Grandpa's bills and Kyle could go home.

Kyle held back a smile, not letting on to Chris that he was excited about the possibility of gold on the mountain. "Why don't you believe the gold part of the story?"

Chris positioned himself to take a shot at the basket. "Well, I know there's gold all over the valley, but there's only a handful of stories that say that any of the Fifty-Niners ever found anything more than a few ounces of gold in their mining claims," said Chris, as he watched the ball swoosh through the hoop. "For years, the rumors have been floating around that one of your mountain miners found the mother lode. But I think the amount of gold gets larger every time someone tells the story. You know, kind of like the story about the fish that got away."

Chris walked with Kyle down the dirt road to the elementary school where Kyle had promised to meet Kimmie after school. It was a couple of blocks away from the middle school.

"People say the old miner's gold is in one of the caves on your mountain," Chris continued, "but no one has ever admitted to knowing which cave it might be in and unfortunately, one day the miner just disappeared. No one ever saw him again. People in the valley say he died up on the mountain without telling anyone where the gold was hidden."

Kyle's thoughts whirled. *The gold could still be there—on our property.*

"So back to the ghost," Kyle said. He'd hope for almost anything if it meant getting him back home. "Has anyone actually seen the ghost?"

"Well, yeah." Chris quit dribbling the ball and faced Kyle.

"Who?" Kyle asked.

"Tommy's dad," Chris said.

Kyle held his hands up in protest. "Never mind. I've heard enough," he said, shaking his head. "Are you on the basketball team?"

"Yeah, I usually play center," Chris said. They were at the basketball court at the elementary school, and Chris whipped around and made a basket. "You?"

"Not yet. I was captain and point guard on the team back home," Kyle said, catching the ball as Chris passed it to him. Kyle dropped his backpack, and they played one-on-one until Kyle had to meet his sister.

Kyle had worked hard to get a position on the junior high basketball team at home. His height and dexterity were a plus at his age. He moved quickly and had a good eye. He was perfect for point guard. If he was forced to stay here, and he made the team, he knew he would be accepted by the other boys.

The dismissal bell rang at the elementary school. "Gotta run," Kyle said, tossing the ball back to Chris. "Great shootin' hoops with you. How 'bout we do this again? I could use the practice."

"Sounds great. Later, bud."

"Later."

Kimmie came bouncing out of the school, giggling with a few girls. Kyle wasn't surprised to see she had made friends so quickly.

"Kyle," Kimmie called, as she ran toward him. "This has been the greatest day. Nikki invited me to her house for a sleepover during spring break, and Lizzie wants me to come see her new baby chicks. Isn't this the coolest?"

"Yeah, the coolest," Kyle mumbled. He took his sister's books.

"The teacher announced that the school is going to be putting on a musical in the fall. I love musicals," Kimmie squealed. Her angelic voice, combined with her curly, long red hair and petite build, gave her an edge for the part of a damsel in distress.

Just before they left Arizona, Kimmie had been selected to be the lead in the fourth grade musical. She cried for days when she had to give up her part.

"Awesome," Kyle said. He shared his sister's passion for music. He sang and played the drums, but for now, he wanted to spend all his time playing sports. He had the rest of his life to focus on music. "I hope you get the lead again."

About halfway across the playground, on their way to the county road to walk home, the whooping and hollering and the stomping of feet, alerted Kyle that trouble was right behind them.

"Hey, you," Kyle recognized Tommy's raspy voice. "Are you afraid of a little ol' ghost?" Tommy and his buddies laughed and fell all over each other.

"Don't pay any attention to them, Kimmie," Kyle said. "Just keep walking. They're trying to scare us with talk of an old ghost up on our mountain."

"You're not afraid of some old ghost are you, Kyle?" asked Kimmie.

"No. I don't believe in ghosts," Kyle said, loud enough for Tommy to hear. "It's all a bunch of crazy talk. Let's go home, Kimmie."

"Yeah, that's right, Kyle. You'd better get home," Tommy teased. "Go home to your mommy. She'll protect you. All those years of trying to keep people from stealing his gold has made that ol' ghost mean. Oooooo."

This was the second time today Kyle had heard someone mention gold. Now Tommy had his attention. He stopped and turned around. He was about to say something to Tommy about the gold, but when he saw the sneer on Tommy's face, he changed his mind. He turned and continued across the playground. They had crossed over the road before Kyle said a word to Kimmie.

"Did you hear what Tommy said?" Kyle asked. "Chris talked about gold too."

"Yeah, so?" said Kimmie.

"Chris says rumors are that an old gold miner found the mother lode and it's hidden in a cave on our mountain." Kyle stopped walking. "Do you know what that would mean to us if we did find gold?"

Kimmie shrugged her shoulders. "No, I don't," she said. "Besides, didn't Tommy say there was a ghost?"

"What it means is," Kyle continued, "if we find gold on Grandpa's mountain, we can go home."

"I do miss home," Kimmie said, as she twirled her long ponytail. "But how would the gold help?"

"Well, if we find the gold, Grandpa can pay the debts on the ranch and be set for life. Right?"

"Wow," Kimmie said. "You're right."

"Yes," Kyle exclaimed, glad that Kimmie finally got it.

Kimmie put her finger to her chin and pursed her lips. "I don't know if I want to leave Morgan Gulch. I've already made some great new friends, and it's so pretty up here with all the trees and the mountains. It's much nicer than the city."

"With or without your help—ghost or no ghost—I'm going to find that gold," Kyle exclaimed. "I want to go home."

# 2

# GHOST OR NO GHOST

All the way home, Kyle chattered about the gold and what it could mean to the family. *What perfect timing*, he thought. Spring break would give him time to snoop around.

Before walking those last hundred yards to the ranch house, they stopped at the rickety wooden bridge that spanned the river from the county road to the road to their ranch. The river was still low, barely covering the large rocks in the riverbed. Over the next month or two, the waters would get rougher and faster with the spring runoff. During the peak of the runoff, the water came up through the gaps in the planks before receding again. Every year, Grandpa worried that this might be the year the bridge would be washed away.

Kimmie jumped up onto the edge of the bridge and waved her arms in the air. "Oh, my sweet prince. When will you rescue me from the evil ogre?"

Kyle bowed, making way for her with a sweep of his arm as she walked along the bridge. He reached up and helped the princess off the edge, as if rescuing her—then they both burst out laughing. She was certainly a drama queen. Kyle threw a rock in the river, then they headed up the hill.

When Kyle and Kimmie got home, Mom was sitting at the kitchen table sipping on a cup of hot chocolate. Mom didn't work, at least not at a paying job. Back at home, she worked in the community doing service projects, helping the homeless, and making dinners for people who were sick or for those with newborn babies. Mom had said she thought this move to the mountains would be good for the whole family to meet new people and get involved in the community. Kimmie went to tell Mom about her new friends and the fall musical, and Kyle headed to his room. As he passed the den, he heard Dad and Grandpa talking.

"We are behind on the taxes and the mortgage, Dad." Kyle knew that tone in his dad's voice; he was about to deliver more bad news to Grandpa.

Grandpa would be heartbroken if they lost the ranch—they all would be. Five generations of Morgans have lived on this ranch. Kyle had heard the stories about how his great-great-grandpa, Charles Morgan—or Gramps as everyone called him—and his family had settled here during the Colorado Gold Rush of 1859. Gramps and his family were on their way to California to get in on the gold mining when he heard the miners had found gold in the valley, as well as copper and silver. He decided to stay in the valley and try his luck at gold mining.

Gramps was well liked by everyone. He knew a lot about mining and agriculture, and lots of other things, so the town asked him to help with just about everything. Gramps helped get several big mines developed, and helped people with their farming. The town began to grow. After a while, the people decided to change the name of the town—the valley became known as Morgan Gulch.

Dad continued, "We can hang on a bit longer, a month or so, but I'm afraid I don't hold much hope in salvaging the ranch."

Grandpa leaned back in his old leather chair sitting next to the fireplace. He stared into the low burning fire, shaking his head. Kyle loved that fireplace. The rocks used to build the massive hearth came from the mountain and turned out to have some nice quartz and bits of topaz on the surfaces of the rocks.

Kyle and his family had come to the ranch every summer since he was young. Grandpa had taught him to fish down at the Williams Fork River. He'd learned to paddle a canoe the summer of his eighth birthday, and he helped raise two colts. But best of all, he loved to come to the ranch to look for treasure. He wasn't anxious to make it his home forever, but the thought of giving up the property upset Kyle.

Kyle went to his room, threw his backpack on the bed, and slumped down into the old wooden chair at his desk. If only he could find that gold. If only there was some gold. He had to find it. It was the only way they could save the ranch. Dad's job paid well, but trying to catch up on Grandpa's bills was more difficult than even his dad had thought it would be.

Kyle's favorite thing to do when he visited the ranch was to dig for gems and look for treasures. As he thought about it, after spending a few summers treasure hunting on the mountain, he couldn't think of any place where there would be lots of gold. There were caves on the mountain, but he had been told never to go into them. *The gold has to be in one of those caves!* He thought. He hoped his parents would think he was old enough now to go spelunking.

Grandpa had introduced him to treasure hunting. Ever since then, he went digging as often as he could. On the weekends back home in Arizona, he rode his bike to his favorite places to dig. When Kimmie was old enough, she started tagging along. She loved the pretty colors and the sparkling gems. Over the years, their collection of gems and old trinkets had grown to be quite large.

Kyle was sitting on his bed, thinking about the gold when Grandpa walked by.

"Grandpa," Kyle said, as he hopped up to catch Grandpa before he went into his room. "Can I ask you something?"

"You betcha, my boy," Grandpa said. Kyle knew Grandpa was trying to hide his worries about the ranch. He always did his best to keep a smile on his face around Kyle and Kimmie. But Kyle knew better. "What can I do for you?"

"I heard some stories at school today about the property," Kyle said, as he plopped back onto his bed.

Grandpa sat next to him. "What kind of stories?"

"Well—" Kyle wasn't sure how he was going to explain to his grandpa what he had heard. "I had kind of a run in with this boy at school. He kept teasing me about a ghost—a mean ol' ghost—on your property."

Grandpa laughed.

"What's so funny, Grandpa?"

"Those old ghost stories have been floating around this valley for years." Grandpa looked out the bedroom window. "You know, for a long time I believed them.

Every once in a while, things would happen that made me think the ghost really did exist."

Kyle's ears perked up. "What kinds of things, Grandpa?"

"Well," said Grandpa, "one night I was sitting in the living room watching television when the rocker on the other side of the room started rocking."

Kyle rubbed the goose bumps on his arms and shuddered. "And?"

"There were a few mornings when I went to the shed to get my tools, and they weren't where I had put them."

"Come on, Grandpa. We all know you forget things sometimes," Kyle teased. "Maybe you just forgot where you put them."

"Well, I often thought that too. But—"

"But what?" Kyle asked, leaning forward.

"But there is one tool I keep in the shed in one particular place. It's a rock pick that belonged to my grandpa—Gramps, as you call him. I believe it's the one he used to pick for gold. I used it occasionally when I went out for my evening walks up the trail. I took it with me to pick at some of the large rocks to see if there was any gold in them. I thought it would bring me good luck."

"Why haven't you ever told me this before? Man, this is important stuff," Kyle said, hardly able to sit still. This meant that there really could be gold here on the ranch. "So what happened?"

"One year, on Gramps's birthday, I was out on my usual evening walk, and I had done a little rock picking. I came back to the shed and wiped the pick clean, as I always did, and put it in its particular place." Grandpa paused and looked out the window again.

Kyle leaned over and looked out the window to see what Grandpa was looking at. Nothing unusual caught his eye. He thought maybe Grandpa was thinking about Grandma. They loved the sunsets up here on the mountain. On some nights, the entire valley turned fiery red. Grandma thought they were beautiful.

"The next day, I went back to get the pick—and it was gone."

Kyle's eyes widened with excitement. "Did you ever find it, Grandpa?" Kyle asked.

"I did," Grandpa said. "I found it lying next to the rock outcropping where I picked for gold. You know the one—the outcropping up the trail just before the big bend that takes you to the other side of the mountain."

Kyle remembered it well. He had been up there a time or two, picking at it himself. It had some topaz in it, and he thought he had seen some amethyst too.

The backside had a large quartz vein running through it, and Kyle knew that more often than not, a person could find gold where there was quartz.

"Well, my boy," Grandpa said. "I never did find any gold, and the chair never rocked by itself again. Sometimes I wonder if it could have been Gramps trying to tell me something over and over again, and I wasn't listening."

Kyle's thoughts bounced around in his head. Even though Grandpa never found any, Kyle was convinced there was gold on the mountain. So where was it, and how much was on the mountain? Would he be able to find enough to help Grandpa? Would he be able to find enough to resolve all the problems and get back home?

"Well, my boy, it's your bedtime. It's getting close to mine too." Grandpa stood up and headed toward the door. "Remember, we've got the big Spring Fling picnic tomorrow. Your mom made her famous lasagna, and chocolate chip cookies. We don't want to be late for that, do we?"

"No way." Kyle stood up and gave his grandpa a big hug. "Thanks for telling me your stories."

"Good night, Kyle," Grandpa said, giving Kyle one of his famous winks. "Don't let the ghosts spook your spirit." With a nod, he was off to his room.

"Wait, Grandpa," Kyle hollered, as he followed Grandpa to his room. "Do you know who Tommy is? He's the one that told me the ghost stories today at school."

"Tommy Dunham?" Grandpa asked.

"Not sure. I don't know his last name."

"I do believe, my boy, that he's a long lost cousin," Grandpa said. "But that's a story for another day."

"Maybe that's why Tommy was so angry," Kyle said under his breath. "What does he know about this mountain?"

"What did you say?"

"Oh, nothing," Kyle said. "Good night, Grandpa. See you at breakfast."

Kyle ran back to his bedroom and shut the door. "There has to be more to this story than just the gold," Kyle whispered, "and I believe Tommy has a version of his own."

Just before going to bed, Kyle went to Kimmie's room and knocked on the door. "Kimmie? Are you still awake?"

"Yes," she said, yawning. "It's hard to sleep with all the creaking of these old wood floors. Are you guys running a race out there?"

As Kyle stepped into the room, he felt the refreshing breeze of the cool spring night coming through

Kimmie's drafty window. The old pine door creaked as he closed it behind him.

"I'm going to go look for that gold," whispered Kyle.

Kimmie rubbed her sleepy eyes. "Kyle, how do you know what Tommy said is true?" she asked. "He doesn't look like a very nice boy."

"He hasn't been nice to us so far," Kyle said, "but it sure seems like he thinks he has a good reason to be mad at us."

"Like what?" Kimmie asked, as she fluffed up her pillow.

Kyle took a deep breath. "Grandpa says Tommy is a long-lost cousin," he said. "I'm thinking that the reason Tommy is mad has something to do with the gold that people say is on our mountain."

"Wow," Kimmie exclaimed, as she sat straight up in bed.

Kyle jumped up onto the big four-poster bed, which stood about two feet taller than any normal bed. Great-grandpa Morgan had made the bed for his daughter using the pine trees from the mountain. It certainly fit Kimmie's princess image. "Grandpa told me a couple of stories, and I'm convinced there's gold here."

"Did Grandpa say anything about the ghost?"

"Well," Kyle said, "he told me a story about a chair that rocked by itself, and a misplaced pick that used to belong to Gramps Morgan. I think it's all his imagination. I can't explain the chair, but I think maybe Grandpa just forgot to put his pick back where it belonged in the shed."

Kyle stood up and stared out the window. "We have that picnic thing tomorrow in town. So tomorrow night when we get home, I'm going to get all my treasure hunting gear together so I'm ready to head up the trail on Sunday. I'm going to find the gold."

"Can I go with you?" Kimmie asked. "I'd love a great adventure."

"Sure," Kyle replied. "But don't you have a sleepover at Nikki's tomorrow night?"

"Yeah, but there'll be lots of sleepovers," Kimmie said. "But how many real treasure hunts does one get to go on in a lifetime?"

"Not many," Kyle said, as he walked to the door. "Do you think you're up for the hike? The mountain is steep."

"You bet I'm up for it," Kimmie said, as she crawled back under the covers. "I can't think of a better reason to get me to the top of that hill."

"Good night, Kimmie. Sleep tight."

Kimmie snuggled deep into her pile of pillows and the lumpy pile of stuffed animals. She pulled the feather comforter up over her head. "Good night."

# 3

# MORGAN VERSUS MORGAN

As the family arrived at the old Williams Fork Clubhouse, the Spring Fling was well underway in the park behind the clubhouse. The Spring Fling was held every year to celebrate the town's history. A jazz band was playing, and flames were roaring out of the barbeques where some of the men were cooking hamburgers and roasting chickens. The children were off playing games, and the ladies were walking around looking at the fruits and jellies, and the pies made for the baking contest.

Kyle and his family had been living in Morgan Gulch less than two weeks. But as they arrived at the Spring Fling picnic, Kyle's mom acted as if they had lived there for years. She had already made many friends. Kyle listened as his mom walked through the crowds asking people how they were doing, or asking if their sick child was feeling better. She was always concerned about everyone but herself.

Dad carried Mom's lasagna over to the food tables, then went to join the band. Dad played the tenor saxophone, and after relentless prodding from Grandpa, he had agreed to play in the band. Fortunately, Dad played the saxophone very well and loved jazz.

Kyle looked around, hoping to find Chris. He saw Kimmie and her new girl friends giggle and toss their hair at the boys as they walked by. Kyle chuckled but at the same time felt a pang of jealousy. He wished he were home again with all his friends—laughing and enjoying the flirtations of the girls, especially after his basketball games.

"Ugh," Kyle groaned, as he saw Tommy across the park. He was harassing another poor innocent kid from school—flipping his head and pinching his arm. *When was he going to quit picking on everybody?*

"Glad to see you made it."

Kyle turned around just in time to get a high-five from Chris. "Did you bring your basketball?" Kyle asked. "I spotted a court at the far end of the park."

"No. My mom made me leave it at home. She said it wouldn't be very sociable to play basketball during the picnic." Chris plopped down on a picnic bench.

"Seems like a perfectly sociable thing to do with the guys."

"The best kind of sociable thing," Kyle chuckled as he gave Chris two thumbs up.

"Gosh, I hate these things," Chris complained. "There's so much girl stuff going on like pie cook-offs, canning contests, and flower stuff."

"No kidding," Kyle said.

"But I do like the pie-throwing contests," Chris said. "Especially when Mrs. Groves is the target. Last year, I hit her square between the eyes. I can just see all the war heroes turning over in their graves at the way she teaches those history lessons."

"Why can't they have good stuff at these things like a basketball game between the girls and the boys?" Kyle asked.

"Yeah," Chris agreed. "That would be awesome. We'd show them a thing or two."

"Show them what, smarty pants?" Tommy was standing uncomfortably close behind Kyle.

Kyle turned around. "What do you want now, Tommy?" Kyle asked. "I'm not going to let you bully me like you do all the other kids."

"Oh yeah?" Tommy stepped closer to Kyle.

Kyle didn't budge. He was about four inches taller than Tommy, and he used that to his advantage. "I'm not sure what's bothering you," said Kyle, "but I wish you'd quit being a bully. You're always picking on somebody."

"What bothers me, Kyle Morgan," Tommy said, as his face turned red and his fists tightened, "is that you and your family think you're all high and mighty in this town. I'm a Morgan, too, and don't you forget it."

Kyle scrunched his face at Tommy. "You're not a Morgan, Tommy, you're a Dunham," said Kyle. "And how would you know anything about my family? We've only lived here two weeks."

"Your family's lived here a lot longer than that," Tommy said.

"That doesn't mean you know anything about my family or anyone else's for that matter," said Kyle.

"And I am part Morgan. My mother was a Morgan," Tommy said. "We have just as much right to the gold as you do—maybe even more."

"What gold?" Kyle asked.

"You know exactly what—what I'm ta—talking about." Tommy's hands shook while he wiped the sweat off his face. "My papa Morgan found that gold. And your family stole it."

Kyle realized that his thoughts about why Tommy was mad might be right. "I'm not your enemy, Tommy, and I doubt our great-great grandpas were enemies," he said. "I don't know anything about any gold."

"You might as well be my enemy," accused Tommy. "Our families had a deal. But your great-great-grandpa knew there was lots of gold in that claim and figured out a way to take it from my papa Morgan."

"Where'd you hear that story, Tommy?" Kyle asked. The Morgans had always prided themselves on being honest people. He couldn't imagine Tommy's story was true. "How do you know what happened between them?"

"Because my family said it happened."

"Of course," Kyle said, "and I suppose your family talks to the dead?"

"Are you calling my family liars?" Tommy argued.

"Isn't that what you're calling mine?" Kyle asked. Kyle couldn't prove anything to Tommy about what did or didn't happen between their great-great-grandpas, but Kyle would do his best to find out the truth. And Tommy had shown him the connection.

If Tommy's family had any rights to Gramps's mining claim, it would be only fair that they would get a share of any gold that was found on the mountain. If they didn't have rights to it, he needed to find the truth to protect his grandpa's interest.

"Tommy," said Kyle. "I'm sure you're only interested in doing what's right for your family, but don't you think it's a little bit out of our control?"

"No, and I'm going to prove you're wrong."

"Ready, Chris?" Kyle asked, ending the dead-end conversation with Tommy. "Let's go shoot some hoops. I've got my basketball in the car."

Kyle turned back to Tommy. "Sorry, Tommy," Kyle said.

Kyle and Chris left Tommy standing all alone, looking like he didn't have a friend in the world. Kyle felt awful.

*How could something like this have been ignored for so many years?* Kyle wondered. *Does Grandpa know?*

"You okay?" Chris asked Kyle. "He seemed a bit uptight. Do you believe his story?"

"I don't know. It doesn't make sense to me." Kyle looked back at Tommy. "But something's got him all riled up."

"Well, for now, let's forget it. We've got a basketball game to play." Chris reached into his pocket and pulled out a handful of coins. "Nickel a basket?"

"Prepare to lose all your money," said Kyle. "I'm feeling lucky today."

# 4

# MAPS AND MOUNTAINS

Kyle had a great time shooting hoops with Chris. A few other boys, who had been watching from the sidelines, joined them on the court.

"Great game, Kyle," said Chris, when the game started to break up at dusk. "I can see why you were the star of your team in Arizona."

"Thanks, bud," Kyle said. "I didn't realize how much I missed playing. Does Ute Park have a good team?"

"We ranked first in the region last year," said Chris. "We didn't do so great this year. One of our best players moved to California. After he left, we couldn't keep up the momentum. We placed third—not so bad. But after you've been regional champs, it doesn't feel so great."

"You just wait 'til I make the team," bragged Kyle. "We'll be number one again."

"Yes," Chris said, as he and Kyle jumped to their high-five. "We're number one."

"Gotta run, Chris. See ya later."

"Later, bud."

Once back at the ranch, Kyle went straight to his room and dug into his closet. He pulled out his maps and spread them out on his desk. Over the past few years, he had collected maps of every place he had been treasure hunting. He was consistently successful in identifying where gemstones could be found. Now it was time to identify where the gold would be.

He searched for the Morgan Gulch map. Grandpa had given it to him last summer. It was old and ripped a little around the edges, but it was his favorite. Grandpa had never said where he got the map, but Kyle suspected it belonged to Gramps. He carefully rolled the map out on his desk, using some of his favorite rock specimens to hold the corners down. For a moment, he imagined life as a miner, hunting and digging for treasure, as he looked over the old map and saw the mining markers.

He sat back in his chair and stared out the window at the mountain. How exciting it would have been to walk up the streams and pan for gold, or find those rare caves that hid golden treasures. All that digging, the shoveling, and then—the ultimate discovery. What a life.

The rock outcropping where Grandpa said he picked for gold was marked on the map. It was an hour's hike from the ranch house, up a winding, steep trail. On one side of the trail, about halfway to the outcropping, there was a large ravine. Kyle and Grandpa had hiked up the trail a couple of summers ago, but they never made it to top.

Kyle studied the map a little longer and put flags on the map where he thought there might be gold. One spot in particular caught his eye. About a half mile from the rock outcropping, further up the trail, there was a cave indicator. *How did I miss that before?* He picked up his red pen and drew an arrow pointing to the location of the cave. "That's where we'll find the gold."

The cave was located in the mountain that Grandpa had named Old Baldy, the tallest peak on their property. It was a beautiful mountain, covered in a carpet of pine trees, except for the peak. Old Baldy's peak was above timberline, covered only in dirt, rocks, and scattered bushes. Grandpa said it looked like the top of a bald man's head.

He kept tapping his finger on the cave marking on the map. Kyle figured this was the cave where the old miner was looking for a large quartz vein, hoping it was full of gold. If there was any place on the mountain that had pockets of gold in those veins, it would be that cave. *It's the perfect spot.* He thought.

He looked at the clock. It was getting late. He had promised Grandpa he would take care of the horses and clean the stalls before he went to bed. Kyle sat at his desk for a few minutes longer, wishing he didn't have to be bothered with chores, but he always kept his promises. He knew if he didn't help, there was no chance he would be allowed up the mountain to look for gold. His parents would make him clean horse stalls until his own head looked like Old Baldy.

As Kyle was sweeping out the stalls, he glanced up the ridge. It was dark, but he could still see a bit of the mountain in the bright moonlight. So much had happened over the past few days. He caught himself looking forward to being here for a long time.

"What am I thinking?" he asked himself. "I can't stay here. I have people counting on me back home." He kept sweeping, and then it dawned on him—he had people counting on him here too.

He finished cleaning the stalls, fed the horses, and headed back to the house. He thought about the ghost stories he had heard and suddenly got the chills. He felt like there was somebody or something following him.

His legs wouldn't move fast enough to get back to the house where there was light—and live people.

"What's wrong, my boy?" Grandpa asked, as Kyle burst through the back door almost knocking him over.

"No—nothing. Why?"

"You look like you've seen a ghost," Grandpa said, chuckling. "Was it Gramps or maybe it was his partner? Now what was his name?"

What a thing for him to say at a time like this. "No. No ghost," Kyle said, trying to stay calm. "I'm anxious to get back to my maps. I'm planning our hike up the mountain."

Grandpa smiled. "Uh-huh. Good night, my boy," he said. "I'm going to bed. I ate too much of your mom's lasagna at the picnic. I can hardly stay awake. See you in the morning."

"Good night, Grandpa."

Kyle could hear Grandpa chuckling as he walked up the stairs to his room. Grandpa loved to git one's goat, as he always said.

Kyle ran up the stairs, two at a time, and shut the bedroom door behind him. He grabbed his green backpack out of the closet and threw it on the bed. He used it only for treasure hunting. Inside was a small pick, a headlamp, a couple of old dental picks used to pick around gems, and a few small brushes for sweeping away the dust. A small shovel hung through a loop on the side of the backpack. In the outside pocket was a bag for their treasures, a compass, a water bottle, and a magnifying glass. He also packed a small book and a science kit with chemicals that helped him identify some of the gems or minerals they dug up.

He knew the hike would be a long one and that Kimmie would get hungry. As quietly as he could, given that every floorboard in the house creaked, he tiptoed to the kitchen to grab cheese and cracker snacks from the cupboard. He turned to go back to his room, then stopped and smiled. He opened the pantry and took out Kimmie's favorite snack—chocolate almond candy bars. He grabbed a few extra just in case she got really hungry.

Kyle put his backpack by the bedroom door. He changed into his pajamas and crawled into bed. He looked out the window. The moon shined brightly on Old Baldy.

"I wonder if there are such things as ghosts?" he asked himself. Just as he was ready to roll over and go to sleep, Kyle saw a small light drift across the side of the mountain. He sat straight up. What would anybody be doing on the mountain in the middle of the night? Who would be up on the mountain in the middle of the night? No one should be out wandering around this late at night—especially on Grandpa's mountain. The light continued across the hillside for a few seconds longer, then disappeared as if the hillside had swallowed it up.

Kyle tossed and turned in bed, unable to sleep. *No, there are no ghosts,* he thought. Even the squeaking of his bedsprings scared him. He yanked the covers over his head. "There are no ghosts," he said. "There are no ghosts."

# 5

# TAPAWINGO

**K**yle tossed and turned all night and didn't get much sleep, but he was still up early and had finished his chores before the sun peeked over the mountain. He looked up at Old Baldy still curious about what—or who—he had seen from his window. He shuddered. Trying not to think about it anymore, he went back into the house.

Back in his room, he went straight to his desk, planning to take one more look at the map before putting it into his backpack.

*It was gone!* He knew he hadn't put the map away before he went to bed the night before, and he hadn't touched it this morning before he went out to the stables. Kyle swallowed hard. He slowly scanned his room—no map. He looked under the desk—no map.

Then, out of the corner of his eye, he saw the map by the door. It was leaning against his backpack, tightly rolled up with one strand of twine tied around it. Kyle's hands started to shake, then his knees, then his whole body shook with fear. *This can't be happening,* he thought.

He took a deep breath, then picked up his backpack and the map. There had to be a reasonable explanation for all of this. "Maybe I walk in my sleep," he mumbled. "Yes, that's it. I walk in my sleep. There are no ghosts."

He flung the backpack onto his shoulder, took one last, hesitant look around his room, and then quietly walked to Kimmie's room.

"You ready?" Kyle whispered through the door. "Gold's a-waiting."

"So is the ghost," came the reply from inside. Kimmie opened her door and stood there looking like a big piece of pink bubble gum. She never went anywhere without matching clothes. She had to look perfect from head to toe. Her pigtails were tied up with fuzzy pink ribbons, which matched the pink daisy pattern on her T-shirt. Her light pink jeans had darker pink trim around the front pockets while the back ones donned pink flowers to match the shirt. Even her socks were pink to go with her pink tennis shoes. Her school backpack and even the small backpack she carried with her on their treasure hunts were pink. She would never get lost in these mountains in that outfit. "Do you think the old ghost will like the shoes?"

Dizzy from all the pinkness, Kyle shook his head. There he stood in clothes with more holes in them than a block of swiss cheese. The only thing on him that matched were the blue of his shirt and his dark blue eyes. He headed downstairs. "Why couldn't I have had a brother?" he grumbled.

"I heard that," Kimmie said, scurrying to catch up with her brother. "You love me. I know it."

When they got outside, Kyle looked past the trees and up the ridge, squinting at the bright sun. He stepped around to the side of the house and turned, taking in the full, panoramic view of the ranch.

Kyle loved the history of the mountain. When Gramps first settled on the mountain, he built a log house, barely large enough for his family of four. Then he added a barn for a couple of cows so they could have milk, and a coop for a few chickens for eggs and meat. That was plenty for them while the children were young.

After Gramps had lived on the mountain for about a year, he befriended a few of the Indians who lived in the valley. Gramps invited them to visit and meet his family. Upon visiting the ranch for the first time, the Indians were impressed by its beauty and the peace they felt while they were on the mountain, they named it Tapawingo—a place of great beauty and joy. They made plans with Gramps to come back and bless the ranch with success and protection.

The Indians returned a few days later in full headdresses. They wore beads and feathers, carried drums, percussion stones, and clay bells to play during their ritual. They danced and sang for hours around a huge bonfire. It wasn't long after that, the Indians were forced out of the valley.

When Gramps's children became teenagers, he built a bigger ranch house, and used the old log house for their guests. The new house stood in the middle of two thousand acres of forest. A white fence lined the property, making it even more majestic than it already was.

Years later, Kyle's grandpa and great-grandpa cleared more trees, and planted grass for their cattle to graze on. They built more outbuildings to store equipment, and feed for the cattle to get them through the winter.

Kyle looked down the ridge from the ranch house at the stables and the outbuildings. Kyle watched as the chickens and a few pigs ran around the stables. What was left of the cattle herd was roaming all over the ranch.

Below the ranch house, over the side of the hill, was the river. Kyle and Grandpa had pulled many fish out of that river. Grandma's garden had sprawled along the riverbank, filled with flowers and many different types of fruit plants. His fondest memories of her were of the two of them picking strawberries—most of which landed in their mouths rather than in the bucket. His mother enjoyed spending time by the river too. She used to spend hours hiding in the trees so she could take pictures of the forest animals as they came to drink from the river.

"I studied the map last night," Kyle told Kimmie. "I know exactly where we'll find the gold."

"If there is any," Kimmie said. "We might just end up getting tired and sore over nothing."

"You don't have to go, you know," Kyle said. "I can do this by myself."

"I know you can, but you won't," she said. "And I know you don't want to. It wouldn't be the same without me."

She was right. They worked well together and always had fun. He was good at reading maps and finding their way around mountains and caves, and she was great at spotting and identifying their treasures.

They stopped at the well to fill their water bottles from the spigot. Kyle checked Kimmie's backpack to make sure it was snug on her back.

"Are you ready for this? We've got quite a climb up the ridge to the cave," Kyle said, as he stared up at the ridge. *I hope this is worth it,* he thought. *Maybe Kimmie's right. Is this going to end up being just another hike? Why should I believe the rumors? I'm just going to be disappointed, and I'll be stuck here forever.* He shook his head.

"Yoo-hoo." Kyle felt Kimmie yanking on his backpack, yelling in his ear. "Are you in there?" she hollered into his ear.

Kyle brushed her away from his ear. "Let's go," he said, as he started walking up the ridge. "If there's gold in those hills, we're going to find it and bring it on home."

"Yee-haa," squealed Kimmie. "Just imagine how many outfits a girl could buy with the gold. So many pairs of—"

"Okay, Miss Beverly Hills," Kyle said, chuckling. "This one's for Grandpa, not for us. So are you ready to get dirty?"

"Oh, I suppose," Kimmie said in her oh-so-grown-up voice. "I guess I could sacrifice a pair of pants or two for Grandpa."

They walked up the ridge, talking about the things they saw along the trail. They watched the squirrels scurry up and down the tree trunks, and spotted a porcupine waddling his way up the mountain. Kimmie made a bouquet from the early spring flowers that lined the trail.

Kyle focused intently on the path in front of them. It was covered in pine needles and an occasional deer track. In his mind, he pictured how the trail might have looked many years ago—bare and worn down from prospectors, small carts, and the Indians.

Grandpa had shared a few mountain stories he had heard over the years. There had been great Indian battles all over the valley. According to the stories, Grandpa's property was the site of one of the biggest and worst of the battles several years before Gramps had befriended the Indians.

"Just imagine, Kimmie," said Kyle. "Indians hunted this ridge." Kyle bent his knees and positioned his arms as if he was an Indian ready to shoot his bow and arrow. He ran behind a nearby bush and cautiously looked from side to side. He darted across the trail to another bush. "He spots the deer drinking from the pond. He sneaks around, ready to shoot. He pulls the arrow back and releases it from his grip. The arrow lunges for the deer."

Kimmie laughed. "I'll bet there are lots of arrowheads up here. I hope I find one so we can add it to our collection."

Over the years, their collection had grown to include rocks, gems, and rusty old railroad track spikes. They had even been lucky enough to find some old coins.

"Hey, Kimmie," Kyle said, as he looked along the ground as they walked.

"Yeah," she said, continuing to pick the flowers.

"If there is gold in them thar hills, as Grandpa says, I'll buy you a chocolate malt if we find gold on this path before we get to the cave."

Kimmie licked her lips and rubbed her stomach. "That sounds so good. You know, big brother, every once in a while you have a great idea."

Kyle and Kimmie continued their hike up the ridge, focusing on the ground, hoping to find some gold. Once in a while one of them groaned with disappointment after a rock with a promise of gold turned out to be nothing.

The farther they walked, the more Kyle thought about the stories that could be told about this old place. Until now, the ground under his feet had only been a place for him to visit for a few weeks a year.

For a brief moment, he had a strange sense of being home.

"Kyle!" Kimmie shouted. "You owe me a chocolate malt."

# 6

## TRAIL TO THE TREASURE

Kyle tossed off his backpack and knelt down beside Kimmie. "How big is it?" he asked leaning closer to Kimmie to get a better look at her find. "Is it a nugget or just some flakes?"

Kimmie rolled the small nugget around in the palm of her hand. "It's beautiful," she said, her eyes as big as silver dollars.

Kyle pulled Kimmie's hand closer to him and squinted as he examined the small treasure. "It's a gold nugget all right," he said.

"I've never seen a real piece of gold," she said. "It looks just like the pictures in our books. Does this mean there's a lot more gold?"

Kyle stood up. He put one hand on his hip and rubbed his chin with the other. "It means there is gold up here, or was at one time."

Kyle knelt down again and picked through the rocks where Kimmie had found the nugget. "These rocks came from higher up the mountain," he said. "They're like the rocks up the trail around the outcropping."

Kimmie scrunched her nose and tilted her head. "Aren't all the rocks the same on the mountain?"

Kyle shook his head. "Mostly," he said, "but mountains are usually made up of several different types of rocks."

"Oh," said Kimmie. "So how do you think these rocks got all the way down here?"

Kyle thought for a moment as he looked up the trail, then back to the pile of misplaced rocks. "If the mining rumors are true, I think the miner's cart tipped over or his pack ripped open," he said, "and the rocks spilled out onto the trail. That means—"

"That means," Kimmie interrupted, "someone was mining for gold up on the big mountain. It means we're gonna find gold in them thar hills."

They laughed. Kyle put the nugget in one of his plastic bottles and put it in his backpack.

"All this excitement," Kimmie said, as she smacked her lips and rubbed her hands together, "has made me hungry."

Kyle pulled the candy bars out of his backpack. "I brought some snacks," he said, waving the candy bars in front of Kimmie's face.

"You brought me a chocolate candy bar with almonds," Kimmie said. "Two great treasures in one day!"

As Kimmie settled down on a tree stump along the trail, she saw something odd in the ravine down below the trail. "Kyle, what's that?" she asked.

Kyle looked over the edge, then dug into his backpack. "Darn. I forgot my binoculars," he groaned. "I can't see it very well. Looks like some kind of old crate. Grandpa probably left it down there and forgot about it."

"Here, use mine." Kimmie pulled her binoculars out of her backpack and gave them to him.

Pink. Of course. They had to be pink. "I hope nobody sees me using these."

"They work better than yours that are back at the house, don't they?" Kimmie asked.

"Yeah, they work just fine," Kyle said reluctantly as he scanned the ravine.

"Can you tell what it is?"

"It looks like," Kyle paused. "Remember what I said earlier?"

"Yeah," answered Kimmie. "So?"

"Well," Kyle said, "you found an old mining cart."

Kimmie squinted down at the ravine trying to get a better look.

He handed the binoculars to Kimmie. "Here, take a look."

Kimmie looked through the binoculars to the ravine down below. "I've seen one of these in my history book," she said. "Do you think that could be the cart that tipped over and spilled the rocks out?"

Kyle looked down into the ravine. "If that's what happened. It's in just about the right spot in the ravine to have tipped over here," Kyle said, as he pointed to the loose rocks on the trail, "and when the miner lost control, the cart rolled down the hill into the ravine."

Kyle looked up at the cave, then down to the ravine. *What happened? Who was pushing the cart? Was it his great-great-grandpa? Was it his partner? Wow,* he thought. This adventure was getting better and better.

"Do you think maybe somebody got hurt?" Kimmie asked. "Do you think it was Gramps?"

"I don't know, Kimmie," Kyle replied. "It's possible. I doubt we'll ever find out."

Kimmie grabbed Kyle's arm. "Why don't we go down there and see what we can find?"

"Oh, I don't know, Kimmie," Kyle said, scratching his head. "It's too steep, and I really want to get up to the cave today."

"We have all week to get to the cave. It's not like we—or the cave—are going anywhere."

Kyle scoped out the side of the hill. It was covered with loose, sharp rocks and thorny bushes. The hillside was too steep to walk down. There would be a lot more sliding than walking. Down the trail a few feet, there were trees that marched their way down to the ravine. He knew they were not going to make it down to the bottom without a few scrapes, but using the trees to hold on to every few feet would save them from getting hurt. The last thing he needed was for Kimmie to get hurt.

Kyle sighed. "You're right, Kimmie," he said. "But be careful. Mom and Dad will tan my hide if you get hurt."

"Yay!" squealed Kimmie.

Kyle walked down the trail past Kimmie, and pointed to the treed area. "We'll go down the hill over there," he said. "Are you going to be able to get back up okay?"

Kimmie rolled her eyes. "I'll be fine, worry wart," she said. "I've done this before, remember? I should have worn my blue jeans. The dirt doesn't show up as much on them."

"This isn't a fashion show, ya know."

Kimmie twirled around and swung her hips from side to side. "One never knows. A girl should always be prepared and look her best."

"The only thing that will notice you up here would be Sammy Squirrel," Kyle said. "But I think he leans more toward the brown tones."

Kimmie scowled. "Are you ready?" She asked, making her way to the trees. "There's a cart waiting for us at the bottom of the hill with a story to tell. Time's a-wasting."

Before he could say a word, Kimmie was quickly making her way down the mountain, weaving in and out of the trees, and giggling all the way to the bottom.

Kyle followed his sister down the hill. *This isn't so bad,* he thought, as he tripped and landed face first in front of the cart.

"Look at this, Kyle," Kimmie exclaimed. "Look at these old tools."

Kyle looked up from the dirt. Right in front of his nose was a rusty pick and a hammer. Underneath the cart was a miner's soft felt cap with a metal plate in it. The plate started at the brim of the cap, bent upwards along the front of the cap. The plate then bent back and was attached to the top. The metal plate was designed to hold a candle, which was a miner's source of light in the caves. *These can't be Grandpa's mining stuff,* he thought as he rubbed the dirt off his face.

"I can't believe this," Kyle said. He stood up and brushed the rest of the dirt off his arms and clothes. "This is almost as good as finding the gold."

Kimmie shook her head. "I don't think so, Kyle," Kimmie said. "I can't buy a darn thing with these tools."

Kyle rolled his eyes. "Oh, brother," Kyle said.

Kimmie scowled at Kyle.

Kyle grabbed the pick and looked closely at the pointy end. "Somebody was picking at rocks for a long time," he commented. "The point is almost worn flat."

Kimmie poked at the felt hat with a stick. "Does that mean they were digging a long time because they weren't finding any gold?"

Kyle picked up the hat and put it on his head. "What I hope it means is that they were digging for a long time because they *were* finding gold."

Kimmie couldn't stop giggling. "This *is* as good as finding gold," she said. "Now we just need to find where they were digging, and we'll be rich."

Kyle put the pick and the hammer into his backpack. "Let's take these back to the house and show Grandpa," he said. "I'd like to ask him if he knows anything about these tools or the cart. I think Grandpa knows a lot more about this mountain than he's telling me."

Kyle and Kimmie sang all the way home. They'd found the trail to the treasure.

# 7

# A WALK WITH GRANDPA

"I knew you loved hunting for gems and trinkets, but I didn't realize how serious you were about all this," Grandpa said, after Kyle finished telling him about what happened on the trail. "I thought you were trying to keep yourself busy so you wouldn't be bored."

"Grandpa, it's awesome," said Kyle. "Ever since Tommy made his wisecracks about the ghost and the gold, I was hoping to prove him wrong. Now, after finding the tools and the old cart, I hope to prove him right. This will end up being the greatest treasure hunt of all times. I can feel it in my bones. Besides that, if the rumors are true, it makes an awesome family legend."

Grandpa chuckled. "Well, my boy, we have quite a walk ahead of us to start you down the road to the rest of the story," he said. "We'll leave at dawn tomorrow. On the way there, I'll tell you what I know."

Kyle scrunched his eyebrows. "Where's there?" he asked.

"You don't want me to spoil the mystery, do you?" asked Grandpa.

Kyle ached for his grandpa to tell him more right then, but knowing his grandpa, the story would be kept a secret until they were on their way at daybreak.

That night, Kyle couldn't sleep. His imagination was going crazy thinking about what he would find with Grandpa in the morning. So far, he had been surprised by everything that had happened here at Morgan Gulch. He knew tomorrow wouldn't be any different. Whatever Grandpa was going to show him would be fantastic. Kimmie was going to be mad that she missed this part of their adventure. She had decided to go to Nikki's for the sleepover, since Kyle had decided not to go back to the cave the next day. The sleepover would be no match for Kyle's outing with Grandpa. Girly giggles or ghostly gold? No comparison.

Kyle stared out his bedroom window, hoping for another sign that he was on the right track to finding the gold and learning more about the ghost. He thought about the taunting comments Tommy had made right before spring break. *Tommy's family believes something bad happened between the two families and that my fam-*

*ily was at fault,* he thought. *What could have been so bad that three generations of a family still hold a grudge?*

He shook his head. He didn't believe there was any truth to Tommy's accusations. The Morgan family's Scottish heritage spoke for itself. There was no way any Morgan family member could ever act any other way than responsible and kind.

His last thoughts of the night turned back to the mountain. *What are you hiding up there, Ghost of Morgan Gulch?* Exhausted, Kyle finally drifted off to sleep.

The next morning, Grandpa strolled into the kitchen as Kyle was inhaling his last bite of breakfast. "Grandpa, your breakfast is getting cold," Kyle said. "I got up early and made eggs and bacon. They'll give us some protein and energy for our hike."

"My goodness," Grandpa groaned as he sat down. He picked up the newspaper and sipped on a cup of hot chocolate. "It's tough for an old man like me to be up before the roosters."

"What are you talking about?" Kyle said. "The roosters have been doodle-doo-ing for hours. They've already had their morning nap."

Grandpa peered over his newspaper. "Those roosters never could tell time."

Kyle felt like he was watching a movie in slow motion. He shifted from one foot to the other wishing Grandpa would eat—and eat fast.

Grandpa took a bite of his eggs. "These eggs taste delicious, Kyle. Where'd you learn how to cook?" he asked. "If you were using your scout training, my eggs would have dirt and twigs mixed in with them."

"Okay, Grandpa," Kyle said. "Quit stalling. This is torture. I'm dying to know what's out there."

Grandpa got up from the table and put his dishes in the sink. "Well, I'd better go get my walking stick."

"Grandpa."

Grandpa turned and winked at Kyle. "Be back in a minute, my boy."

Kyle quickly cleaned up the kitchen, grabbed his jacket and baseball cap, and ran out the door. Behind him, the old screen door swung back and forth, squeaking. The wooden porch sagged in spots, and there were gaps in the planks. He watched two chipmunks run out from under the porch, obviously scared by the noise. He paced back and forth on the porch.

He shoved his hands into his jeans pockets. "How long does it take to find your walking stick that's always by your headboard?" Kyle asked under his breath.

Finally, Grandpa stepped out onto the porch. "Ready, my boy?" With his walking stick in hand and his hat on his head, Grandpa started down the road.

"Am I ready?" Kyle asked. "I was wondering if we would get out of here before I became a ghost on the mountain."

Grandpa chuckled. "Oh, I'm a little slow at times, but I'm not a snail, you know," he said. "The story of Morgan Gulch has been sitting on that mountain top for many years. It's not likely to go anywhere anytime soon."

"Yeah, I know," said Kyle, stopping in the road. "Hey, Grandpa. Aren't we supposed to be heading up the trail to the cave?"

Grandpa kept walking. "You can if you want, but what I want to show you is this way."

Kyle caught up to his Grandpa. They walked about a half mile down the road from the ranch house, then Grandpa took a sudden turn into the bushes. On the other side was an old wagon road that obviously hadn't been used for many years. It headed off along the side of the mountain and disappeared down the hill. *How did I miss this?* Kyle thought.

Grandpa put his arm around Kyle's shoulders. "Let me tell you a bit about your family, my boy," he said. "It will make your treasure hunt all the more interesting."

As Grandpa and Kyle walked, Grandpa told him a story that had begun about 150 years ago. Grandpa confirmed the parts of the story that Kyle had heard about how Gramps and Tommy's great-great-grandpa came to settle in the Morgan Gulch Valley.

"As you already know," said Grandpa, "your great-great-grandpa and Tommy's were brothers and very good friends. Their father was the first Morgan to arrive in America from Scotland. Thomas—Tommy's great-great-grandpa—and Charles Morgan were a wild pair. They were always scheming some crazy idea. They came out west to strike it rich. Their original plan was to go to California and get in on the end of gold rush, but they decided to stay here in the valley. The valley was not a well-known place. There were only a few other men here with their families struggling to survive."

"How did Gramps know there was gold on the mountain?" asked Kyle, eager for more of the story.

Grandpa sat down on a large boulder and wiped his forehead with a hankie. "Whew," he said. "It takes a lot more to hike these mountains than it did in my younger days."

Kyle sat down next to Grandpa. "Yeah, I could use a rest too."

"He didn't know," Grandpa continued. "It was all quite by accident that they found gold. The brothers

## THE GHOST OF MORGAN GULCH

settled on adjacent properties—Tommy's great-great-grandpa's property was on the other side of Old Baldy. They were in the process of building Gramps's home when they found gold in the river. Their theory was that it washed down from the caves in the mountain.

"As the years went by, the brothers made their living working in the copper mines. But their hearts were in gold mining. They spent as much time as they could in the caves. The rumors say they had small pieces of gold assayed from time to time, but nothing significant.

"Tommy's great-great grandma couldn't take the hardship, so she took their children back to Boston. Convinced that someday he would strike it rich, Thomas stayed in the valley to work and regularly sent money back to his family.

"For many years, Thomas and Charles spent time helping the other families build up the valley. Because of the work that your great-great-grandpa did for the people in the valley, they renamed it after him. He took care of everyone including Tommy's great-great-grandpa."

Grandpa drank some water and shared some with Kyle. He stood up, adjusted his hat, and they started up the road again.

Tommy's great-great grandpa became sick and died. After that, Gramps was rarely seen in town. His own family didn't see him for days at a time. One day—he never came home. Grammy Sara passed away shortly after that.

"I know Gramps is buried with Grammy Sara down by the river under the big pine tree," Kyle said, "but if he never came home, how did he get buried next to Grammy?"

Grandpa's chin quivered. "Some of the other miners found him in an old cabin the brothers had discovered on one of their outings. They were the ones that brought him down the mountain to be buried. They said it looked like Gramps laid down on his bed one day—and died. They also found Thomas's grave. He is buried across the stream from the cabin."

Kyle scrunched his nose as he always did when he was deep in thought. "It doesn't sound like there was any fighting going on between Gramps and Tommy's great-great-grandpa," he said. "Do you know why Tommy's family is so angry with us?"

"No," Grandpa said. "I don't know why or how the families grew apart. I do know that ever since Tommy's great-great-grandpa died, the two families have not spoken to each other."

Grandpa stopped walking. "This is where I leave you to your mystery, my boy."

"Aren't you going with me?" asked Kyle.

## THE GHOST OF MORGAN GULCH

Grandpa put his arm around Kyle's shoulder and gave him a squeeze. "No, this is your hunt," he said. "I'm too old to be digging around in the dust and the rust. Go find out the legacy your great-great-grandpa left to you and your family. Follow the road up and around the bend another hundred yards. I hope you find what you're looking for and you have the courage to find the truth; I never could." Grandpa turned and walked away, whistling his favorite tune—"O My Darling, Clementine."

Kyle stood and watched until Grandpa was out of sight. He turned and stared up the hill—his heart pounded. He wasn't expecting to do this alone. He took a deep breath and marched up the road. Right about at the hundred-yard mark, Kyle stood staring down a gentle slope from the road at a broken-down small cabin. At that moment, Kyle knew that whatever was inside could be the key to unlocking the greatest mystery ever known to Morgan Gulch.

# 8

# THE CABIN

The old cabin gave Kyle the creeps. Kyle was tempted to turn and run, but he knew he had to find out what happened to Gramps and his gold. "Here goes nothing," he said.

The bottom of his pants and shoes were wet by the time he reached the cabin after walking through the damp, tall grass. The rickety old building was surrounded by trees and thick, thorny bushes which stretched as far as he could see. Kyle figured the door was on the other side of the cabin and the only way to get to it was to climb through the tangled mess. He shivered with each step, wondering what might be lurking in the bushes. Kyle's arms flailed about as he burst through the bushes into a clearing.

"Ewww," he shuddered, as dead bugs and sticky twigs went flying into the air as he brushed them from his hair and clothes.

A few yards away from the cabin door, and sitting next to the stream, was a log table, and two chairs made from tree stumps. Just as Grandpa had said, across the stream and up the hill a few feet, was the grave of Tommy's great-great-grandpa, Thomas. Kyle shuddered.

Using some of the bigger rocks in the stream as stepping stones, Kyle hopped across and walked up to the rock headstone. Kyle read the crudely written inscription—

> *Thomas McMillan Morgan*
> *Dearest brother and friend*
> *Rest in Peace*

Kyle took off his cap and spent a few moments in silence out of respect for Thomas Morgan. He wondered if Tommy had any idea his great-great-grandpa Thomas was buried up here.

Kyle hopped back across the stream and walked up to the cabin door. He grabbed what was left of the doorknob and counted to three. He took a deep breath and slowly opened the door wondering what mean or scary creatures of the forest might be lurking about inside. The door stuck on the warped floor. Kyle leaned against the door and pushed hard. The door broke loose and flew open, taking Kyle with it. He fell flat on his face a few feet from an old pine bed. His heart pounded against the floor.

Kyle stood up and looked around the room. The cupboard doors were hanging off rusty hinges, parts of the roof had fallen down, and rusty tin cans lined the shelves. Spider webs covered every corner, and birds had taken up permanent residence in the rafters. There were holes in the walls and in the floor where animals had made their way in and out of the cabin.

The idea that Gramps died on this bed made Kyle uncomfortable. Kyle wondered what might have happened to Gramps and why he died. Was he sick? Was he hurt? As Kyle walked over and stood beside the bed, he was overwhelmed with a familiar presence. He turned to see if anyone was standing behind him. No one was there.

In the far corner, along the same wall as the bed, were two chairs and a table made out of scraps of wood. On the table, covered in dust and cobwebs, held down by fist-sized rocks, were small piles of yellowed papers.

Kyle sat down at the table. "Wow," he said. "This is awesome." Kyle started sorting through the papers. The ink had faded on most of them, so it was difficult to see any details. Never in a million years did he ever think one of his treasure hunts would turn out to be so mysterious with so many twists and turns.

After spending a long time looking at the papers and not being able to read most of them, Kyle was tired and frustrated. Needing to stretch his legs, he walked to the middle of the room and stared at the bed. Suddenly, an image of a man appeared, leaning on the bedpost. Kyle rubbed his eyes then looked back at the bed. The man was gone. *I must be really tired,* he thought.

Kyle went back to the table and moved his chair to the other side of it so he could keep his eye on the bed. As he sat down, he noticed the room was getting darker. He looked out the small cracked window and saw the clouds gathering about the mountain. A light rain began to fall.

He knew he didn't have much time to get back to the ranch before a storm set in. Though he couldn't read much of the writing, he finished looking through the papers quickly to make sure he didn't miss anything important. In his excitement to get out the door that morning, he had left his backpack at the house, so he decided to leave the papers rather than risk getting them wet on the walk home.

He slumped in his chair, disappointed. He had found nothing to prove Gramps had found gold or where he had been digging. *Maybe this was a wild goose chase after all,* he thought. Even though he was discouraged, he knew he would have to come back and go through the papers again. Next time, he'd have his lighted magnifying glass to help see the faded writing more clearly.

Kyle walked over and stood next to the bed. "Well, Gramps," he said, as if Gramps was sitting next to him. "I'm not sure what happened up here or what clues you've left, but I'll be back to find the answers. I need to help Grandpa, and your gold is the only way I can do that."

He looked around the room, taking in all the details and looking for any other clues before he left. "You must have been very sad when your brother died. I'll be back up with—"

Something shiny, lying beneath the floorboards, caught Kyle's eye. He stuck two fingers in the small hole in the boards. Using them like tweezers, he grabbed the object and pulled it up through the hole. It was a gold nugget ring.

He jumped up from the floor and shouted, "I knew it. They did find gold." He shoved the ring into his pocket and walked out of the cabin, yanking the door closed behind him.

Kyle crawled through the thick brush and walked up to the road, then turned and looked back at the cabin. The rain stopped, and the sky started to clear.

"Yeeha," he shouted, as he raised his arms into the air and shook them. "Kimmie is going to be so mad at me."

# 9

## BOCA GRANDE

"Are you still pouting over the cabin thing, Kimmie?" The hike to the top of the mountain had been a quiet one.

Kimmie stomped her foot and dropped her backpack. "I can't believe you went up there without me."

"I'm sorry, Kimmie," said Kyle. "I had to go. Spring break is only a week long. We need all the time we can get to search for the gold. Besides, we'll go back to the cabin, and you can help me look through the papers. You really haven't missed anything."

Kimmie tossed her hair and crossed her arms. "No, just finding a gold nugget ring."

Kyle sat down on the rock outcropping. "I left everything the way I found it. It will be just like finding it for the first time."

"It doesn't make me feel any less left out," she whined.

Kyle picked up his backpack. "So are you ready? Or do I have to go cave exploring by myself?"

"Of course, I'm ready," said Kimmie. "I didn't hike all this way just to get all sweaty. I have a stake in this game too, you know."

"Great. Let's go," Kyle said.

Kimmie picked up her backpack and heaved it onto her shoulders with a great sigh. "Hey, why didn't you talk to Tommy about what you found in the cabin?"

"I want proof of what really happened," Kyle said, "before I tell Tommy anything. He can be mad at me for a few more days."

"I'll bet you become a politician when you grow up."

"What?"

"You heard me," said Kimmie. "Let's go."

Kyle unrolled the old map and showed Kimmie the red marks he had drawn on the map. He had high hopes about coming home at the end of the day with the loot. "Here's where the cave is," he said. "And here's where we are—next to the rock outcropping."

Kimmie pushed the map away. "You know I can't read maps—all those squiggly lines confuse me," she said. "I'll follow you. That way when you fall into some large cavern, I'll be able to tell Grandpa where to find you."

"Funny," said Kyle.

Kyle didn't know how big the cave was, if it had any tunnels, or if there were any large caverns, as Kimmie pointed out, that would be a problem for them. *What have I gotten us into?* He wondered. He hoped he would be able to find the hidden treasure and get his sister home in one piece.

He rolled up the map and put it into his backpack. "We're close to finding the Morgan family fortune, Kimmie," he said. "What do you think about that?"

There was no response. "Kimmie? Where are you?"

A faint noise came from behind him. Kyle turned to find Kimmie crawling out of the side of the mountain, coughing and covered in dirt.

"Are you all right?"

"I was swal—lowed up by that mountain," gasped Kimmie, as she shook her hair and tried to wipe the dust from her clothes. "And just look at me. My clothes are ruined."

"You can get new clothes," Kyle said, helping Kimmie to a rock to sit down. "Are you okay?"

Kimmie rubbed her eyes and dusted off her lips. "Yes, I'm fine. I tripped over that tree root and fell head first into the side of the hill," she said. "I may not be able to read maps very well, but I don't think that huge hole is anywhere on your old map."

"No, it isn't." Kyle pulled the map out of his backpack and unrolled it again, looking more closely at the symbols and trail markings. "The cave we're looking for is still another hundred feet up the trail. I don't see anything on this map showing an opening next to the rock outcropping."

Kimmie shook the dirt out of her shoes. "That cave has one big mouth. From what I saw, it goes way back into the mountain. It's huge."

"Boca Grande," Kyle said, as he snapped his fingers. "It just came to me."

"What are you talking about?" Kimmie peered over Kyle's shoulder to look at the map. "I don't see any Boca Grande on that map."

"No," said Kyle, scrunching his eyebrows together and rubbing his chin. "It's possible that when this map was made, Boca Grande hadn't been discovered."

Kimmie grabbed the map. "Well," she said, as she rolled it up and handed it back to Kyle. "It's discovered now. So let's go spelunking."

"Spelunking?"

"You know, cave exploring."

"I know what it means," said Kyle. "I didn't think you knew what it meant."

Kimmie tossed her hair. "Humpf."

Kyle dug through his backpack and pulled out two large pieces of chalk and his headlamp. "Put your headlamp on, Kimmie, and put this chalk in your pocket."

"What's the chalk for?"

"We'll use it to mark where we've been in the tunnel," said Kyle, "just in case we get lost."

They put their headlamps on and secured their gear. Kyle's palms were sweaty, and his heart was pounding. He wasn't sure if it was more in anticipation of finding the hidden treasure or being afraid of getting lost. He shuddered. Kyle still wasn't sure he believed in ghosts, but thought he should be ready—just in case.

Kyle took a slow, deep breath and walked to the opening where Kimmie had fallen. As he crawled through the branches and vines that were still covering part of the opening after Kimmie's fall, a blast of cold, damp air hit his face. As he scooted further into the hole, he felt something brush against his cheek. Kyle shivered.

"Are you okay?"

"Yeah," Kyle groaned. "I'm good."

He adjusted his headlamp. Kimmie was right—the cave was huge. He helped Kimmie through the entrance, pushing away the branches and leaves to make it easier for her to get through the opening. Once she was inside the cave, he made sure Kimmie was okay, then he brushed the leaves and dirt from his face and arms.

"This is really amazing," said Kyle. "I didn't expect this." The cave was damp and musty. He felt a chill as he stepped further into the center of the large room.

Kimmie scanned the big room. "Where do we start, Kyle?" she asked. "You didn't happen to find a map that tells us which tunnel to take, did you?"

"No," answered Kyle. "I wish I had. I'll bet every one of these tunnels has its own tunnels and on and on. It's going to take forever to find the gold."

"Well then, we'd better get started. As much as I'd like spring break to go on forever and ever, it's gonna end soon."

He looked at each of the entrances to the tunnels. "Okay, let's start with the middle one," he said, pointing to the dark hole directly in front of them. "It'll probably take us the deepest into the cave, and if I learned anything about geology, that's where we'll find the largest quartz veins and the biggest pockets of gold."

Kimmie gave Kyle a thumbs-up. "Not too shabby, big brother. Makes sense to me."

"Get your chalk ready, Kimmie. We'll mark the walls about every ten feet, alternating sides—just in case."

Kimmie tilted her head. "Just in case what?"

"I'm not sure," said Kyle. He checked his backpack one more time. "Did you check your gear? Do you have water and matches?"

"Kyle," said Kimmie. "Quit stalling. We'll never find the gold standing here in the middle of this room. We have to go into the tunnels sometime."

"I'm not stalling," said Kyle. "I just want to make sure you have everything you need."

"Just in case?" Kimmie teased.

"Well, yeah."

Kyle grabbed Kimmie's hand and walked toward the center tunnel. The closer to the tunnel they got, the tighter Kimmie squeezed Kyle's hand. He smiled. She was not the only one who was afraid.

# 10

## HANSEL AND GRETEL

Kyle hoped that they had picked the right tunnel that would lead them directly to the gold, but the middle tunnel was only about fifty feet deep. The second tunnel wrapped around into a different tunnel, and the third tunnel kept winding around and around, seemingly with no end—or beginning. Kyle had no idea where they were.

After winding through the endless tunnel for a long time, Kimmie stopped and yanked on Kyle's arm. "Are you sure we're not lost?"

"No, I'm not sure," said Kyle. He looked at his watch and realized that they had been wandering around the cave for about two hours. "Have you seen any of our chalk marks lately?"

"No, not for a while."

"Not sure if that's a good thing or a bad thing."

"Well, it might mean that we finally quit walking around in circles," Kimmie said, with a slight grin. "Or it might mean we're totally lost and won't ever get out of here."

Kyle scrunched his eyebrows and looked up and down the tunnel. "We'll be fine," he said. "All we need to do is find at least one of our chalk marks again, and we'll be able to get back to the entrance."

Kimmie asked, "And, big brother, what if we don't find any of our chalk marks?"

"We'll keep walking until we do," said Kyle. "What's the worst that could happen?"

Kimmie folded her arms and rolled her eyes.

Kyle shook his head and put his arms up in surrender. "Don't answer that." He took off his backpack and started going through his gear.

"What are you looking for?" asked Kimmie.

"My compass," Kyle answered. "The entrance to the cave is east of the ranch house. So we need to be heading west to find our way out of here. I don't know why I didn't think of that earlier."

"Wow," said Kimmie. "That's twice today you've said something that made sense. Be careful, Kyle, someone might think you know what you're doing."

"Well, I wouldn't be jumping to that conclusion," said Kyle. "The compass may not work in the cave. There might be too much interference."

"What kind of interference?"

"Certain types of metals can cause a compass to read incorrectly," said Kyle. He opened the compass and waited for the needle to settle. It pointed to north then moved back and forth between north and south. Kyle turned toward the tunnel wall. "We have to head that way."

"When did you turn into Houdini?"

"I may have to be Houdini to get us out of here," Kyle said. "We'll need to wind our way around and find the tunnels that keep us heading west. We'll eventually make our way out."

Kimmie took a deep breath. "Okay, I'm ready. Let's get out of here."

Kyle packed up his gear and secured his backpack on his back. "I'll keep my eye on the compass, and you watch for our chalk marks. If we're going in the right direction, we should see them."

Kyle and Kimmie headed west, as best they could. Some of the tunnels seemed familiar, but they saw no chalk marks.

After a while, Kimmie stopped and rested against the tunnel wall. "Are you sure that compass thing works?"

"No, not really. But it's all we have right now," said Kyle. "I'm sorry, Kimmie. I didn't mean to get us lost."

"Are you kidding? This has been so cool," said Kimmie. "I'm not worried. We'll find our way out. What fun would it be if we didn't have a little bit of trouble?"

Kyle nodded. "You're right. I was just hoping to get in and get out. No problems, no troubles and home with the gold by sundown."

Kimmie laughed. "You are so predictable. Only you would think we could walk right into Boca Grande and walk out with Oro Grande," she said. "We'll find the gold, Kyle. I know you'll figure it out. You always do."

Kyle burst out laughing. He had been so focused on finding the gold and solving all Grandpa's problems, he had forgotten to have fun. They always had fun on their treasure hunts—even if they didn't bring home any treasure. It was all about the adventure.

"Well then," Kyle said with a bit more confidence. "Let's get out of here."

It took another thirty minutes for Kyle and Kimmie to find a tunnel with their chalk marks on the wall.

"Kyle," said Kimmie. "Something is very wrong. It looks like something—or someone—has tried to erase our chalk marks. Forget what I said earlier. This isn't fun anymore. Someone is following us."

"That's not possible," Kyle said. "We would have heard noises if there was someone else in the cave."

"Why else would our chalk marks be so smudged?" asked Kimmie. "We didn't brush up against them as we passed. Something else did. And honestly, Kyle, I don't want to find out what that something else is anytime soon."

Kyle put his arm around Kimmie and gave her a squeeze. "Let's just keep walking. I'm sure there's a good explanation for all this."

Kimmie's this-ought-to-be-good look burned a hole in Kyle's head.

"I'm looking forward to hearing the story you're going to make up once we get out of this tomb," she said.

"Everything's going to be fine, Kimmie," he said. "If someone is following us, they are probably trying to scare us, not hurt us."

"And you know this how?"

"Because, if they wanted to hurt us, we'd be—" Kyle stopped talking.

"That's comforting," Kimmie groaned. "And if it's a ghost?"

"If it's a ghost, it can't hurt us, and it can't smudge chalk marks," Kyle said with a grin.

His grin quickly changed to a frown as he stared at the smudged chalk. He realized that for whatever reason the chalk marks were smudged, he didn't want to come face-to-face with that reason while they were still inside the cave.

"Let's get out of here," Kyle and Kimmie said at the same time.

"It looks like we're heading in the right direction," Kyle said. "We need to keep following the chalk marks all the way out."

"Are you sure?" asked Kimmie. "We did that earlier, and we ended up going around in circles. I think someone's messed with our chalk marks to lead us away from the cave entrance. Someone wants us lost in here."

Kyle was once again surprised at his sister's thinking. "Let's try to ignore the chalk marks and use the compass and our instincts to find our way out." As quickly as he could, Kyle stabilized the compass and regained his bearings. He started walking and motioned to Kimmie to follow.

"Well, I'm glad your instincts are better than mine," she said, hanging on to Kyle's sleeve.

"Let's hope they're good enough."

Carefully, they made their way through the tunnels, and just when Kyle thought they were home free, they came to a juncture where the tunnel split out into three different tunnels. The compass went wild. Kyle pointed it toward each tunnel and everywhere in between. The needle would not settle on one direction long enough for him to get a reading.

"Kyle, please don't tell me you don't know which tunnel to follow."

"No," Kyle replied. "I would never tell you that. I just thought it would a good time to take a break."

"Ha-ha," said Kimmie. "What are you going to do?"

"Well, here's where the instinct kicks in," Kyle said. "Give me a minute, and I'll figure it out."

Kyle looked from one tunnel to the next and back again. A movement caught his eye in the tunnel to their right. He turned to see if Kimmie had noticed it, but she was busy flicking dust from her clothes. Kyle looked back to the tunnel. For a moment, Kyle thought he saw the figure of a man gesturing to him to follow him. A part of Kyle wanted to run the other direction, no matter where it took them, but Kyle's instincts told him to follow the man.

"I know the way to the entrance, Kimmie," Kyle said. "Follow me."

In less than five minutes, they were looking at the most beautiful sight ever—the outside of the cave. Kimmie giggled and Kyle wiped the sweat from his forehead. He had more research to do before they came back to the cave—but he knew they would be back.

On the way down the trail, Kyle thought about what—or who—he had seen in the cave. Had he seen the ghost of Morgan Gulch?

# 11

## A SECRET ENTRANCE

"First dibs on the bathroom," Kimmie yelled, as she ran down the last stretch of the trail. "I have to get out of these icky clothes and take a long, hot bubble bath."

It would be hours before Kimmie would be out of bubbles, so Kyle headed to his room to clean up his backpack and get ready for the hike back up the mountain in the morning.

After rearranging his backpack, putting everything back in its place, Kyle stopped and looked out the window at the mountain. In his mind, he retraced his steps, trying to figure out where he went wrong in the cave. How did he get so turned around? What—or who—had he really seen up there? Kyle wasn't ready to admit he had seen the ghost of Morgan Gulch. He unrolled the map and laid it out on the desk. He knew the map didn't show the tunnels, but he felt strangely drawn to it to continue the search for the gold.

Kyle was interrupted by a knock at the door. "Come in."

Grandpa opened the door and nodded toward Kyle's gear on the bed. "So you had quite an adventure on the mountain today, eh?" he laughed. "Kimmie was squealing about it all the way into her bubbles."

Kyle stood up and walked over to the window. "It was awesome, Grandpa, even getting lost was pretty cool. But I know you haven't heard the best part of the story."

"What do you mean?" Grandpa asked, walking over to Kyle's desk. He sat down and began studying the map sprawled across the desk.

Kyle pulled up a chair across from Grandpa and sat down. "What I mean is—I saw somebody in the cave."

Grandpa grunted and continued studying the map.

Kyle waved his hand in front of Grandpa's face to get his attention. "Grandpa," he said, "I-I think it was Gramps."

Grandpa didn't respond.

"Of course, that means I'd have to admit that I believe in ghosts," Kyle said. "Anyway, whoever it was helped us find our way out of that cave. I'm not sure if

I would have been able to get us out of there without some help."

Grandpa peered over his glasses at Kyle. "How close were you to the entrance when you saw Gramps?"

"We were very close. But if I hadn't seen him and followed him out of the cave, we might still—" Kyle realized what Grandpa had asked him. "I knew you believed in Gramps's ghost. I knew it."

Grandpa turned his attention back to the maps. "I trust you would have found your way out—eventually," he said.

Kyle walked around and stood behind Grandpa to get a better view of the map. "Why do you think Gramps was in the cave?" Kyle asked. "Do you think he wants us to find the gold, or do you think he knew we needed help?"

"I'm not sure about the gold, but from what I've heard about Gramps," said Grandpa, rubbing his chin, "he was always very attentive to his family's needs. I doubt even the grave could stop that."

Kyle walked over and leaned on the windowsill. He was beginning to realize the importance of the mountain and the ranch—the significance of what Gramps had accomplished here. It had meaning for the family and the valley.

Kyle turned back to Grandpa. "What are you looking for?" he asked. "Do you think there's something on the map that might help us find the gold?"

"No, not that I can see," said Grandpa. "I was just looking over the maps to see if there were other entrances besides your Boca Grande, as Kimmie called it. But other than the one marked on the map and Boca Grande, I don't see any."

"I think Boca Grande is the better choice," Kyle said. "According to the map, that location is prime for finding gold. The other cave doesn't appear to go deep enough into the mountain."

"Well, you could be right," Grandpa said, as he straightened up the maps. "I hope—"

"Grandpa," Kyle interrupted. "You're wearing Gramps's nugget ring. That's awesome."

Tears welled up in Grandpa's eyes as he looked at the ring. "It's one of the few things we have from Gramps. It's quite a tribute to his legacy."

Kyle held back his own tears. "Yes, it is."

"Are you ready to go back up the mountain tomorrow?" asked Grandpa, as he headed toward the bedroom door.

"Yes," said Kyle. "I hope Kimmie's ready bright and early."

Grandpa laughed. "You have quite a handful with that sister of yours. She's a pistol."

"She's a trooper, Grandpa. She keeps up with the best of 'em," Kyle said. "But she does get a bit feisty about her clothes and her hair. Geesh."

"Well, you get a good night's sleep, my boy. Good night."

"Good night, Grandpa," Kyle said, as the door closed behind his grandpa.

Despite being tired, Kyle tossed and turned in bed for a while. Putting the sleepless hours to good use, he got out of bed and went to his desk to study the maps again. He looked at the area around the cave entrance and around Boca Grande. Boca Grande definitely was the best choice. But what if there was another entrance—a secret entrance—that Gramps might have used once he found the gold? An entrance most people wouldn't find—one Gramps used so he wouldn't have to go through the maze of tunnels inside Boca Grande.

Kyle chuckled. If Gramps wanted the secret entrance to remain a secret, he wouldn't have marked it on the map. Kyle sat back in his chair and closed his eyes, recreating their search in his mind. He and Kimmie hadn't gone northwest of the big entrance. They hiked southeast around the mountain and stopped looking for any other caves after Kimmie had stumbled into

Boca Grande. Could there be a secret entrance to the northwest of Boca Grande?

Kyle dozed off in his chair while contemplating the secret entrances. He woke with a start, catching himself before he fell to the floor. He rubbed his eyes and shook his head. "Ooof," he groaned. "I've got to get some sleep."

As he crawled into bed, he noticed it was raining. He loved it when it rained in the mountains. It brought out the peacefulness of the property. Unfortunately, it meant that he and Kimmie would not be going back to the cave in the morning. The trail would be too slippery to hike. Instead, he would spend part of his day helping Grandpa with whatever he needed done around the ranch. Mom and Dad had gone back to Arizona for several days to take care of some business. While Dad was gone, Kyle was sure Grandpa would need extra help. After that, if it didn't rain too much throughout the night, he might do some fishing.

He smiled. Though he wasn't ready to call it home yet, he could get used to life on the mountain.

## 12

## GOING FISHIN'

Kyle and Grandpa spent most of the morning mending fences and repairing the doors and windows on the stables. When they were done, Kyle rubbed down the horses and put new horseshoes on Daybreak's front hooves. Kimmie came out and pretended to help, but spent more time telling Kyle how to arrange the straw in the stalls and playing with her dolls.

Kyle was pounding the last nail into the horseshoe when Grandpa came into the stable. Grandpa patted Daybreak and gave her a rub on the neck.

"What's up, Grandpa?" Kyle asked.

Grandpa put his hand on Kyle's shoulder. "Well, my boy, it appears that you might be here a bit longer than expected, so I'd like you to have Daybreak—as your horse."

"You mean it? Really?" Kyle asked.

"Yep," said Grandpa. "You have taken care of her every time you've visited, and it seems she's become quite fond of you."

Kyle hugged his grandpa. "Thank you," he said. "I'll take good care of her, Grandpa. I promise."

"I know you will," he said. "Now finish up your work so you can get down to the river and do some fishing. It's a beautiful day for casting out flies. Hopefully, the river is not too muddy after the rain."

"Can I ride Daybreak down to the river?"

"Yep," he replied. "She hasn't been out in a while. I'm sure she'd love the walk, especially with those new shoes of hers."

Kyle chuckled. "Awesome."

Kyle put the tools away and ran into the shed to get his fishing tackle. He knew where most of the great fishing holes were in the river below the ranch, and Grandpa had taught him some tricks to bring in the big ones. The Williams Fork River wasn't on the list of Division of Wildlife's Gold Medal Waters, but in it were some of the largest fish in the entire valley. The only river that could outdo it was the Blue River, just over the mountain. It was a famous Gold Medal river that brought in fishermen from all over to try for the big ones.

"Kyle," Kimmie shouted from across the yard, "can I go with you?"

At first, Kyle was irritated at Kimmie for asking, but he figured there was no harm in taking her with him. Kimmie wasn't much of a fisherwoman. After a cast or two into the river, and getting her line tangled in the bushes, she would go play in the sand along the riverbank.

"Grab your pole," said Kyle. "I've got the tackle box. We'll dig for worms and find some rock crawlers at the river."

"Thanks, Kyle," Kimmie said skipping off to the barn.

As he came out of the shed, Kyle saw Grandpa rocking in his chair on the porch. "Grandpa," Kyle hollered. "Grab your pole. There's some big fish just waitin' to be caught."

Grandpa was out of his chair in a flash. "Don't need to ask me twice." He saddled up his mare, Chante', and grabbed his fishing gear.

Kyle put Kimmie up on Daybreak, secured the fishing gear on the saddle, and climbed up behind her. "Ready, Grandpa?"

Grandpa climbed into his saddle. "Ready. Let's go."

Though the ride to the river was short, Kyle couldn't remember a more enjoyable one. He had always loved horses. Kimmie, however, was less fond of them. She would never admit it, but the deep impressions she left on Kyle's arms told him she was afraid.

When they got to the bridge, Grandpa pulled Chante' to a stop. "Kyle, let's go down river about half a mile or so. Last fall, I discovered a new fishing spot. I think you'll like it."

"Lead the way," said Kyle. He and Kimmie followed Grandpa down the trail that ran along the river. Kyle had been down this part of the trail only a time or two. He liked going up river from the bridge to do his fishing.

The river was low, and the water bubbled over the rocks. Kyle watched the water all the way down the trail, looking for the occasional flip of the fins as the fish fed on gnats swarming above the water. The squirrels chattered in the pines, sending a warning of danger down the trail, and a deer and her fawn drinking from the river ran off into the forest.

Grandpa stopped and climbed off his horse. He pointed at a large boulder, half in and half out of the river on the opposite bank. "Right there, Kyle."

Kyle got off his horse and helped Kimmie down.

"Whip your line two or three times in the air," Grandpa said, imitating casting his line into the water.

"Then cast it into the water and let it float around the boulder. You'll catch yourself a big one."

"I changed my mind," said Kimmie. "I don't want to fish. I don't feel like getting slimy. I'm gonna go play in the sand by the bridge."

Kyle was not surprised. "Okay. Be careful."

Kimmie skipped up the trail, and Kyle and Grandpa took their poles and tackle off the saddles and walked to the edge of the river.

"It's been a while, Grandpa," said Kyle. "I think I was about nine or ten the last time we went fishing together."

Grandpa pulled his fishing lines through the loops on his pole. "Yep, got rained out the last time, I recall."

Kyle laughed. "Yes, we did. We were soaking wet by the time we got back to the house. We lost all our fish too."

"What a waste," Grandpa said, as he tied his hook on the line. "There was a giant on that stringer. He must have been a ten pounder."

Kyle was ready to cast out his line but thought better of it. He turned to Grandpa. "You go first. Let's see if you can catch Ol' Man trout."

The fishing stories in the valley were always exaggerated, but Kyle's favorite was about Ol' Man trout. Every fisherman in the valley believed they had hooked the oldest and biggest fish in the Williams Fork. No one could ever prove it, but the stories about how they struggled with the ol' fish for hours grew bigger and better every time they told them.

Grandpa whipped his line a few times then cast it across the river and watched as it crossed over the current and swirled around the boulder. Kyle watched his grandpa cast his fishing line over and over again. At that moment, it didn't matter to Kyle if he ever got his line in the water. He'd have plenty of chances to fish, but maybe not so many more fun times with his grandpa. Right now, it was Grandpa's turn, and he seemed to be enjoying every minute of it.

By the time they both had caught three or four fish each, none of which were Ol' Man trout, the sun was low in the sky, and Kimmie was quite restless.

"Can we go home now?" she asked. "I'm hungry."

Kyle looked at his watch. "Wow, we've been here for hours."

Grandpa reeled in his line one last time. "Yeah, my big belly is crying for food too. Are you ready to go, Kyle?"

"Yep," he replied. "Food sounds really good."

Just as they were getting on their horses, it started to rain. Kyle looked at Grandpa and laughed. "It's just like old times, huh, Grandpa?"

Like many of the mountain spring storms, the rain was coming down so hard they could only see a few feet in front of them. By the time they got back to the house, they were drenched. They put the horses in their stalls and the fishing gear in the shed, then ran to the house.

Grandpa was the first one dried off and dressed, so while waiting for Kyle and Kimmie, he cooked up some breakfast for dinner. It was a favorite family tradition for an evening meal. Kyle and Kimmie thought pancakes, bacon, and hot chocolate tasted better at night after a good rain than they ever did for breakfast.

The three of them sat at the table and told stories about things they remembered from Kyle and Kimmie's visits to the ranch. After a while, Kyle realized Kimmie had become very quiet. He had been so wrapped up in telling stories with Grandpa that he didn't notice that she had fallen asleep. Grandpa carried her to her room and put her into bed.

Once the dishes were done and his other chores finished, Kyle sat at his desk and studied his maps one more time. *There's got to be an answer somewhere on these maps. Gramps thought of everything. He found the gold—he knew there was an easier way to get to it. What am I missing?* He thumped his pencil on his head as if trying to knock the answer loose. Would there have been a reason for Gramps to hide the place where he was digging?

"The answers aren't going to jump off the map for you," said Grandpa.

Kyle about jumped out of his chair. "Gosh, Grandpa, you startled me."

"I knocked."

"You did?"

"Yep," said Grandpa. "You were quite engrossed in your old map."

"I've been trying to find any clue that might lead us to the gold," said Kyle. "I'm not finding anything."

"I don't think the answer is on that map," Grandpa said. "If Gramps had found gold, I'm sure he remembered how to get back to it a second time. I doubt he would put the location on the map in plain sight. I'm sure he wanted to keep it a secret."

"Well," thought Kyle, "after being in the cave and getting lost in the tunnels, I don't think there's any way Gramps would have been able to go back the second time and find his way through the maze of tunnels without clues. He had to write it down somewhere."

Grandpa pursed his lips and rubbed his chin. "Yes, and I'll bet he did just what you did—marked the walls so he could find his way out of the tunnels."

"You mean, like with cha—," Kyle paused. "The chalk marks aren't ours."

Grandpa winked at Kyle.

Kyle took a deep breath. "Those smudged chalk marks—belong to Gramps."

# 13

## BACK TO THE CABIN

Kyle stopped shoveling cereal into his mouth and looked out the window at Boca Grande. "Kimmie, I know we decided to go right to the cave today, but—"

Kimmie looked up and stopped mid-bite. "But what?"

"We'll get back there, I promise," Kyle said. "But I want to go back to the cabin."

"Why?"

Kyle pushed his half-full cereal bowl aside. "I think Gramps left some other clues there that will lead us to the gold."

"What's wrong with the map you've been staring at all week?" she asked. "It has all kinds of marks and arrows on it." Kimmie took another bite of her cereal. "One of those squiggly lines should lead us to the gold. And why would you think Gramps left any clues? He knew where the gold was."

"You were in the cave," said Kyle. "You know how confusing it was. All we did was go around in circles and run into dead-ends. There has to be some secret code to the tunnels or a secret—"

"Your imagination's going to get you into big T-R-O-U-B-L-E."

Kyle stood up so fast that his chair fell backward and hit the floor. "That's it, Kimmie. We've got to get to the cabin and find the missing link."

"What missing link?" Kimmie asked. "I thought you went through everything when you were at the cabin the last time? You know, the time you went without your treasure hunting partner?"

"Go on, rub it in. I said I was sorry," said Kyle. "You don't expect me to sit around this house twiddling my thumbs when there's an entire mountain to explore, do you? I didn't know I'd find such great stuff at the cabin."

Kimmie set her hands on her hips. "Absolutely I expect you to sit and twiddle your thumbs. We're partners, mister," she said, as she stomped her foot. "I wouldn't have gone to the sleepover if I had known you were going to take off without me."

Kyle laughed. "You'd better get your gear—and fast—or you'll miss another great treasure hunt."

"What about the secret, Kyle?" asked Kimmie, putting her dishes in the sink. "What about the missing link?"

"I'll tell you on the way up to the cabin." Kyle was already in his room getting his backpack by the time Kimmie caught up to him. Kyle flung his backpack on his back. "Are you ready?"

"Give a girl a minute," said Kimmie, flinging her hair. "I'll meet you out back."

Kyle stood on the porch and scanned the property, left to right and back again. He looked up to Boca Grande. It was rugged, but beautiful. He knew there had to be a clue to help find what was hidden in the mountain. Kyle new Gramps wanted this mountain to belong to his family forever. The Morgans had enjoyed a comfortable life on the mountain for many years, and if they could figure out Grandpa's money problems, the family would be comfortable for many more years, even without the gold. *What secrets do you hide, Boca Grande?* Kyle jumped a little as the screen door slammed behind him.

Kimmie slapped Kyle on the back. "It's okay, big brother. I'm not one of your ghosts."

Kyle rolled his eyes. "Are you finally ready?" He asked. "I could have been to the cabin and back, and off to the fishing hole by now."

"Excuse me?" Kimmie set her hands on her hips. "I stopped to clean up your mess."

"I didn't leave a mess."

"What do you call leaving a pile of sugar on the table and a chair upside down on the floor?"

"Oh yeah," said Kyle.

"Oh yeah is right," said Kimmie. "If Mom came home to a messy kitchen, the only thing we'd be hunting for would be the broom."

Kyle didn't like being wrong. He liked it less when his younger sister was right. "Thank you."

"So," Kimmie asked, putting on her backpack. "I want to know more about the missing link and the secrets."

"Secrets?" Kyle checked Kimmie's backpack.

"Don't tease me," said Kimmie. "Just tell me."

With one last tug on Kimmie's straps, Kyle said, "We can talk as we walk. Let's go solve the mystery of Boca Grande." Kyle started walking up the trail.

Kimmie squinted as the bright sun peered over the mountain. She dug through her backpack for her pink sunglasses and put them on. "Wait for me," she called to Kyle, hurrying to catch up to him. "I want to know more about the secrets."

As they started their climb to the cabin, the early morning chill hung in the air. Kyle took a deep breath.

He loved the mountain air. It was so different than the city smog; so refreshing. "I found some great stuff at Gramps's cabin, but I realized this morning that there's something missing."

"What?" Kimmie asked.

"The one thing that every great treasure hunter needs to help him find the buried loot," said Kyle.

Kimmie appeared puzzled for a moment.

"You know—X marks the spot?"

Kimmie's eyes widened. "A treasure map."

Kyle and Kimmie slapped a high-five.

"It still doesn't answer my question as to why Gramps needed a map to the treasure," said Kimmie.

Kyle paused for a moment. "Gramps didn't need the map for himself," he said. "I think he made one—for us."

Kimmie grabbed Kyle's jacket and stopped him. "What do you mean 'for us'?"

Kyle sat on an old tree stump. "You should have worn your hiking boots," he said, as he watched Kimmie sit down on the ground beside him and shake the pebbles out of her shoes.

"You know nothing about fashion, do you?" Kimmie asked.

"I know that hiking boots go very well with hiking. They make quite a matched pair."

Kimmie snorted and put her shoes back on. "Your humor needs some work too."

"Funny." Kyle stood and helped Kimmie up. "To answer your question, I believe Gramps knew he wouldn't be able to get all the gold out before he died. He made the map so we—his family—could find what he left behind."

Kimmie shrugged. "Makes sense. But if that's true, why hasn't anyone found it after all these years?" she asked. "It seems the cabin would be a logical place to put it. And you'd think he would put it somewhere it could be easily found."

Kyle rubbed his chin. "Well, not too easily found. There's always a disgruntled, unsuccessful miner looking to steal someone else's claim. You know the story," Kyle said, as he adjusted his backpack. "I'm sure he hid it out of sight. But I don't believe he would have hidden it so well that someone who knows where it should be, wouldn't be able to find it. That's why we're going back to the cabin. The map has to be there."

Kimmie looked puzzled.

"We're going back," said Kyle, "because I believe that in the cabin there's either a clue or a map showing us where the gold is hidden."

"Didn't you look everywhere?" Kimmie asked.

"Yeah," Kyle stammered, "I did."

Kimmie smiled and nodded her head. "You didn't find it because I wasn't there," Kimmie said.

"And why would having you there make any difference?"

"You know why," smirked Kimmie. "Women are better finders than men."

"Finders?"

"Yes, finders," she said. "Send a guy to find something, and we have to go back and finish the job."

Kyle shook his head.

Kimmie laughed and slapped her knee. "I know why you didn't find the clue or the gold," she said. "You wanted to get out of there because you were afraid of the ghost!"

"I wasn't afraid," Kyle squirmed. "It started raining and I wanted to get home. Besides, if you had seen what I—"

Kimmie folded her arms and asked, "Seen what?"

Kyle's secret was out. Maybe Gramps would be there again, and she could see for herself that he wasn't just seeing things. "I did see a ghost," Kyle said. "I think I saw Gramps's ghost."

Kimmie peered over her sunglasses at Kyle. "You're serious, aren't you?"

"Yes, I am."

Kimmie looked up the trail and back at Kyle. "Well, let's not waste any more time," she said. "I want to meet my great-great-grandpa."

# 14

## BOX OF TREASURES

Kyle and Kimmie stood on the road looking down into the shallow valley. The tree branches hung over the cabin and yesterday's rain still dripped onto the cabin roof. A mist from the stream drifted over the cabin and down the hill.

"There's Gramps's cabin, Kimmie. What do you think?" asked Kyle.

"I think we're wasting time. Race ya."

Kimmie took off running before Kyle could get a foothold. When Kyle caught up with her, Kimmie was standing in front of the cabin door frozen in her tracks. He knew she was afraid to go into the cabin—afraid to see Gramps.

"Aren't you going to go in?" he asked.

"Well, uh—," she said. "I was waiting for you."

Kyle grinned. "Uh-huh. Afraid to go in?"

"Of course not," she said. "But you go first. You've been in there before. I don't want to mess anything up."

"The place is a disaster. How can you mess anything up?" Kyle put his hand on the door, then hesitated. He wasn't sure if he was prepared to see Gramps's ghost again.

He turned and looked at Kimmie, then turned the doorknob. The door creaked, startling them both. Kyle took a deep breath. "There's nothing to be afraid of."

Kimmie rolled her eyes. "Except the door."

Just like the first time, Kyle had to push hard against the door to open it. Even though it didn't take as much effort, and he knew what to expect, he found himself on the floor, again. "Ooof," he groaned. "Watch your step, Kimmie."

"Really?" Kimmie stepped over Kyle and walked into the cabin. Kyle watched her take in every detail of the room. She walked over to the bed.

Kyle, now standing next to Kimmie, dusted himself off. "So," he asked, "what do you think?"

Kimmie's mouth was wide open, as her eyes scanned the room from top to bottom. There were old tin cans, bottles, a few old pieces of clothing. "I didn't realize there would be so much great stuff up here. I mean, look at all of these old things."

Kyle laughed. "It's all pretty amazing, isn't it?"

"I'd say it's the best treasure we've found yet," Kimmie said.

Kyle turned and walked over to the table. "Come here, Kimmie. I'll show you what I found."

Joining Kyle at the table, she picked up a couple of the papers and looked at each of them. "Even if there is valuable information on them," she said, as she pulled one of the papers up close to her eyes for a better look, "it won't do us any good. We can't read any of it."

Kyle pulled his lighted magnifying glass out of his backpack. "Maybe this will help."

Kimmie put the papers down. "You go ahead. I'm going to look around," she said. "If I'm lucky, I'll find some hidden treasure like the gold ring."

"You're more likely to find something under the floor," said Kyle. "Since the walls are made of logs, there's no place to hide anything."

"You're right about that," replied Kimmie. "I'll start over by the bed."

While Kyle was examining each paper, one by one with his magnifying glass, hoping to see any detail that might give a clue about where the gold was, Kimmie started her search. She got down on her hands and knees, and started knocking on the floorboards with her knuckles, one by one, down one side of the cabin and up the other.

"If there is a map, do you have any idea what it might look like?" Kimmie asked. "I can't imagine it would be like those pirate treasure maps we see in the cartoons. I mean, really—a torn-up piece of paper with an X to mark the spot where the treasure is buried?"

"Uh, no," said Kyle. "I'm looking for something with a little more detail. As much as all of this seems to be a tall tale, I'd say Gramps's map would actually look like a real map. You know, something with those squiggly lines you so dearly love."

"I'll make those stupid squiggly lines my best friends if it will help us find the gold."

"Be careful what you say around here," Kyle warned. "I wouldn't be surprised if those squiggly lines started talking to us."

Kimmie shook her head. "That's just weird."

She stood up and leaned up against the corner of the cabin, opposite the corner where she started. "I usually have better luck than this," she said, kicking a piece of warped floor board. "I would have found the map by now if we were on one of our usual hunts."

Kyle put his magnifying glass down and put his head in his hands, frustrated from the lack of success. "Yeah, I know." He put his hand to his chin and scrunched his eyebrows. "That map is here, I know it is."

She looked over to the bed. "Too bad we can't just ask Gramps."

"Give it a try," Kyle suggested. "He might answer you."

"Oooo," said Kimmie and started her search again.

Knock. Knock. Then a shuffle as she moved over a few boards. Knock. Knock. Shuffle. Shuffle. Knock. Knock. Thud.

"Kyle, I think I found something." She knocked on the boards around the area to make sure she had heard it right. Knock. Knock. Thud.

Instantly, Kyle was kneeling down beside Kimmie looking for a way to remove the boards. "Help me find something to pry this up."

"Okay," she replied. As Kimmie started to push herself up off the floor with her hand, she fell through the floor up to her elbow. "Ouch."

"Are you okay?" Kyle asked, as he carefully pulled the board away from her arm.

Kimmie groaned as she pulled her arm out of the hole and examined it for scrapes. "Yes," she said, picking a few splinters out of her skin.

Kyle looked at her arm. "We should get you home," he said, "and clean up your arm."

Kimmie raised her eyebrows. "Are you kidding? We're so close," she said. "I know it."

She carefully put her arm back into the hole through the splintered boards. "Oooo, yuck," Kimmie said. "This gives me the creeps. There's definitely something down there. Whatever it is, it's covered in spider webs, and it's too big to get through this hole."

Kyle looked around the room. Not readily finding anything to pry the boards loose, he decided to use his hands. "Kimmie, get your flashlight," he said.

Kimmie pulled her arm out of the hole and skipped over to her backpack to get her flashlight. Kyle pulled his sweatshirt sleeves down around his hands to protect them from the splinters. He tugged on the broken board until it came out.

As Kyle was pulling the next board out, Kimmie knelt down and shined the light under the boards. She squealed, "It's like—like a treasure box."

Beneath the cabin floor was a box about one foot wide by one foot long and about eight inches deep.

Kyle hurried to pull out the next three boards. Lying in a hole dug in the ground, the box was made of pieces of wood that were roughly cut and loosely held together with rusty nails. Kyle reached in and lifted the box out of the hole, and put it on the floor.

Kyle stood up and helped Kimmie off the floor. "Let's open it over on the table," he said. He picked up the box and walked over to the table, leaving a trail of dirt and dead bugs behind him.

As Kyle set the box on the table, spiders scurried from the cracks. Kimmie shuddered as he brushed them off the table to the floor. He put his hands on the lid and looked at Kimmie. "Are you ready?"

Kimmie squirmed, "Yes," she squealed. "Open it."

Inside the box, covered in a thick coat of dust, was a gold pocket watch, a pair of spectacles, a picture of two miners, a piece of a pencil, and a few coins lying on top of an old book.

Kimmie picked up the picture. "This must be Tommy's papa Morgan with Gramps. It's a shame it's been buried up here. It should be hanging on the wall with the rest of the family or maybe given to Tommy's family."

Kyle looked at the picture. "I think Tommy would like that."

Kimmie put the picture down and picked up the watch. She took her bandana off her neck and wiped the watch clean. "It's beautiful." She rubbed it a little more until the gold sparkled.

Kyle laid the book on the table and sat down in front it. He brushed the dust off the cover and opened it. The pages were moldy and brittle. Kyle turned the first few pages. "This is Gramps's diary."

Still polishing the watch, Kimmie asked, "How do you know it belongs to Gramps?" she asked.

Kyle turned back to the front cover and pointed to the writing. "His name is written in the upper corner of the inside cover."

"Oh," said Kimmie.

Kyle snapped his fingers. "I bet the map is in here," he said. "Why else would Gramps hide it?"

Anxiously, but cautiously, Kyle continued to look through the book, one page at a time, making sure that if the map was in the book, he wouldn't miss it. Every few pages, he stopped to read the entries. As he turned them, some of the pages ripped, and some of them came out completely. About midway through the book, stuffed into the binding, was a folded piece of paper.

Kyle looked at Kimmie. "Well, what is it?" she asked.

# 15

# X MARKS THE SPOT

Kyle gently pulled the paper out from the bindings. As he unfolded it, he was disappointed to see that it was not a map. It only took him a few seconds, however, to see that they had discovered another important piece of paper. It was a letter from Thomas Morgan to Gramps.

> *My dearest brother,*
>
> *As I lay dying, I ask my last favor of you. Please write to my family and tell them of my fortune. Take my gold and have it assayed and send the money to my family. I leave my property to you for your own use as I have no one here to take care of it. Please bury me at the water's edge where we have spent countless hours panning for our fortune and sharing our life's dreams,*

*one with another. Give my love to Sara and tell her goodbye. Good luck to you, my true and trusted friend.*

*Thomas*

Stunned, Kyle handed the letter to Kimmie. "Read this, Kimmie. It's from Tommy's great-great-grandpa to Gramps," he said. "We have to find the map."

As Kimmie read the letter, she shyly wiped a tear or two from her cheek. "Are you sure there is a map?" she asked.

Kyle leaned back in his chair and hesitated before he answered. "Yes. I'm sure he left a map."

"Maybe someone else has been here and found the map and left everything else."

"No, I don't think so," Kyle said. "When I first got here, it didn't look like anyone had been here for many years."

Kimmie raised her eyebrows. "Someone could have taken it many years ago."

"Oh," Kyle said. "I didn't think about that."

Kimmie picked up the spectacles, and Kyle continued his search through the book. He picked up the book to get a closer look and the back cover fell off.

Looking through Gramps's spectacles now sitting on the bridge of her nose, Kimmie said, "Kyle, it's the treasure map."

Kyle almost dropped the book. "Where?"

Kimmie pointed to the last page of the book, now exposed without the cover. She squealed, "X marks the spot."

Kyle closed the book and looked at the back page. "Oh my gosh, Kimmie," he exclaimed. "We did it. We found the map." Kyle's hands were shaking. He carefully put the book back on the table.

"I can't believe there is an actual treasure map," Kimmie stuttered. "You were right."

Kyle nervously rubbed his hands together. "I'm a little surprised we found it."

Kyle put the box on the floor and laid the stack of papers on top of it. He pulled his old map out of his backpack and laid it out on the table. He set the book next to it, the map page facing up.

Kimmie picked up her backpack. "I'm going outside," she said, as she rubbed her nose. "I need some fresh air."

Kyle didn't look up from the maps. "Okay," he muttered. "I'll be out soon." Kyle traced the trails and elevation lines on his old map, and found similar markings on Gramps's crude map in the book.

Gramps's map showed an X that appeared to be deep inside Boca Grande. "X does mark the spot," he said. He picked up the papers and put them on top of the book. Kyle wrapped them in his bandana, and put them in his backpack along with the other things from the box.

Kyle made his way out of the cabin, making sure not to trip over the warped boards again, and joined Kimmie at the edge of the stream.

"Oh, this is the life, Mr. Morgan," said Kimmie, as she dipped her bare feet quickly in and out of the cold stream. "We should retire from school and be full-time pirates."

Kyle closed one eye, pretending he was wearing an eye patch. "Aye, matey."

"Yo ho ho," Kimmie replied.

"Kimmie, I think I've figured out where the gold is," Kyle said. "We need to get back up to Boca Grande. We are so close."

Kyle lifted Kimmie up and put her on the log table and put her shoes and socks beside her. Kimmie wiped the water from her feet with her bandana and put her shoes and socks back on. She stuffed her wet bandana in her backpack.

"Let's go, Captain O'Malley," exclaimed Kyle.

"Mother lode, here we come."

The hike to the cave seemed exceptionally long. Kyle had discovered a new trail on the map in Gramps's diary that started at the cabin, and joined the trail from the main house about three quarters of the way to the Boca Grande. The first part of the trail was unfamiliar to them, and was difficult to follow. Tall grasses hid rocks and holes in the trail, causing them to trip along the way.

Kyle was ahead of Kimmie on the trail. He slowed to a stop to let her catch up. While he waited, he thought about everything that had happened over the past few days. He knew he would have to work out the trouble between the families before they went back to school after spring break. If any part of the gold or the property belonged to Tommy's family, they were entitled to have it. He needed to find the truth. It was the right thing to do.

"I hate to say you're right," Kimmie panted, "but you're right."

"Right about what?"

Kimmie sat down on the trail. "Hiking boots go better with hiking," she said. "My feet are killing me."

Sitting down next to her, Kyle asked, "Would you like to go home and come back tomorrow making the right fashion statement?"

Kimmie adjusted her shoes and scraped the mud off the bottom with a stick. "Absolutely not. We're so close," she exclaimed. "The hard part of the hike is over. It's all downhill from here."

"Relatively speaking, of course," chided Kyle, "once we get over this last hill. Ready?"

"Yeah, I'm ready." Kimmie started singing. "We're off to see the Wizard—" She skipped on ahead of Kyle as if heading down the yellow brick road to the glittery land of Oz. Kyle smiled and followed her up the trail.

The closer they got to the cave, the colder the air became. Kyle thought about calling it quits for the day. He knew he would be grounded for this life and the next if Kimmie caught pneumonia.

Caves were colder than the outside air, and looking at the condition of the trail, he guessed that there could be snow around the cave entrance. Even though it had only rained at the house, even the slight increase in elevation between the ranch and the cave could turn the rain to snow this time of year. If he had to dig through snow, that meant continuing on with the hunt in wet, cold clothes. He shuddered at the thought. When Kyle caught up to Kimmie, she was standing at the entrance to the cave, fidgeting.

"Gosh," said Kimmie. "What took you so long? Gold awaits us."

Kyle chuckled. "You've been waiting all of thirty seconds for me to catch up."

Kimmie was tapping on her pink watch. "Thirty seconds wasted, big brother," she said. "We could've found the gold and been home for dinner by now."

"Yeah, I wish," said Kyle. "If there's as much gold in that cave as I'm hoping there is, it's going to take all of us weeks to haul it out."

Just as Kyle feared, the cave entrance was partially covered in snow. He hung his thumbs in his belt loops and stared it. Would it be easier to push through the snow or dig it out? He laughed as an idea came into his head.

Kimmie looked up at her brother. "I don't like that look on your face. What are you up to?"

Kyle stepped back and made a run for it. "Geronimo!" He plunged head first into the snow, pulled his body into a ball, and rolled as he went through cave entrance.

# 16

## SECRETS UNEARTHED

Kimmie peered through the hole. "Kyle? Are you alive?" No answer. Under her breath, she said, "A shovel would have been a better way to get through the snow."

"I heard that." Kyle's voice echoed in the cave.

"Aaah." Kimmie tumbled backward as Kyle's head poked up at the edge of the hole. He teased her with an eerie laugh. "You look like you've seen a ghost."

Kimmie shook her fist at him. "You're gonna be a ghost if you keep this up."

Kyle came out of the cave and brushed the dirt and snow from his clothes. Fortunately, he had avoided getting wet except around his shoulders. He could deal with that. "I'd like to find the gold first."

Kimmie closed her eyes and shook her head. "You're so exasperating."

"So are you up for this, or are you going to freak out again?" Kyle knelt down and crawled back through the hole.

"I didn't freak out. You scared me." Kimmie crawled into the cave after him, and called out, "Hey, wait for me."

Once inside the cave, Kyle took his headlamp from his backpack and put it around his head securing it with the elastic band. He turned it on and took Gramps's treasure map out of his pocket to get his bearings.

"Well, what are we waiting for?" asked Kimmie.

"I am trying to match the squiggly lines on the map with the layout of the cave." Kyle studied the map a little harder. "Something doesn't look right."

"What do you mean?"

"Well," Kyle said, "according to Gramps's map, there should be one more tunnel in this cave. The tunnel that leads to the gold isn't here."

"How can a tunnel just disappear?"

Kyle folded the map and put it in his pocket. Hanging his thumbs through his belt loops, he scanned the cave's main room over and over again. *That tunnel has to be here*, he thought. He concentrated on the part of the cave wall where the map showed the tunnel should be. Kyle walked closer to it and began feeling the cave wall with his hands.

"What are you looking for?" Kimmie asked, following him like a shadow.

Kyle kept moving along the wall. "I am looking for the missing tunnel. If Gramps's map says there's a tunnel here," he said, "then I know there's a tunnel here, and I'm going to find it."

"How will you know if you find it?" she asked. "How will we get through it once you find it? How will—"

"Okay, okay." Kyle put his hands up to stop Kimmie's questions. "So here's my theory. See the smudged chalk marks?" he asked, as he pointed to the marks on the wall. "Grandpa and I believe these marks were made by Gramps while he was here looking for the gold."

"Wow," Kimmie said, taking a closer look at the wall. "And?"

"If you follow them along this wall," Kyle said, as he walked, pointing to the marks, "you see where they disappear. So I think Gramps filled in the tunnel entrance, left the map where someone would find it, and made sure he left enough clues behind for us to find the tunnel and the gold."

"Did he leave behind the dynamite and the shovels so we don't have to spend the rest of our life digging through the tunnel?" Kimmie asked. "We ought to find it about the time we are old and gray."

Kyle chuckled. "No, silly, no dynamite required. I think Gramps filled in the tunnel entrance, trying to cover up evidence that someone had been digging here," Kyle said, explaining his theory. "But over the years, sediment and water from above have seeped through the cracks filling in the gaps. Unless someone knew the tunnel was there, and if they don't get real close, the filled in area looks just like the rest of the cave wall."

Kyle pulled the map from his pocket and opened it. His eyes squinted, and he looked up at the cave wall. "If Gramps's map is even close to being accurate," he explained, "the tunnel should be right about—there. Right where those chalk marks end." Kyle pointed to a spot between two of the other tunnels, but off center by a few feet. He folded the map and stuck it in his pocket. He rubbed his hands together, preparing for his next move.

"You're not going to do another tuck and roll into that wall, are you?" asked Kimmie. "If so, we might as well bury you here and now. I'm sure Gramps is close by and could walk you over to the other side."

"Interesting thought, but no," Kyle said. He walked over to his backpack and pulled the shovel out of the side loops. "This time I'll use the shovel. If we poke at the wall long enough, the dirt and rocks will loosen up."

Kimmie frowned. "Ya, it'll loosen up right on top of us."

"Maybe," said Kyle. "Get your shovel. We've got work to do."

Kimmie scowled. "Maybe?" She grabbed her shovel and stood waiting to see what would happened next.

Kimmie shined her headlamp on the wall as Kyle used the point of the shovelhead to poke around, trying to find the right spot to start digging. As he poked, Kyle wondered how difficult Gramps had made this or if it would be easy once they broke through the surface of the wall. How far back did he fill the tunnel? Is the gold right on the other side of the wall? Kyle got chills just thinking about how close he might be to the gold.

"Find anything?"

"Not yet," said Kyle. "But I know we're about to hit pay—"

Kyle's next poke into the wall caused some dirt and rocks to give way. Kyle fell forward, hitting his head on the wall. The force of Kyle's body against the cave wall caused the whole tunnel opening to collapse. Kyle lay, sandwiched between the tunnel wall and some of the fallen ceiling.

"Dirt," Kimmie said, as she stepped through the rubble. "Kyle, talk to me. Are you hurt?"

Without moving a muscle, Kyle responded, "I hate to say you were right, but you were right."

"Oh, you mean that the rocks would loosen up right on top of us?"

Kyle groaned and tried to get up. "Yes."

Kimmie moved what rubble she could off Kyle. "One of these days, you should start listening to your silly sister." She gripped Kyle's arm and helped him up. They made their way over the rubble and back to the stable cave floor.

"That was awesome!" Kyle exclaimed, as he dusted himself off.

"Well, you might rethink that," Kimmie said, "when you are explaining to Mom and Dad how you got that huge cut on your forehead."

Kyle reached up and wiped away the blood. "Ah, it's just a scratch," he said with a big grin. "Besides, it was worth it. We found the hidden tunnel."

Kimmie frowned. "Yeah, but I don't see any gold."

Kyle smiled and nodded. "Today's the day, Kimmie. We're so close to the gold, I can feel it in my bones."

"I'm sure Gramps felt it in his bones, too," she replied, scrunching her eyebrows. "You see where he ended up."

Kyle chuckled. He walked over to his backpack and flung it over his shoulder.

They made their way through the rubble, and once inside the tunnel, Kyle stopped and pulled out the map. He adjusted his headlamp, which had been twisted during his fall, then looked at the map. He compared it to the tunnel.

Looking from the map to the wall and back again, he said, "This is weird."

"What's weird?" Kimmie asked.

"Well," Kyle said, rotating the map side to side. "According to the map, the gold is supposed to be just a few feet in front of us."

Kimmie rolled her eyes. "Then this is all a big joke because I don't see anything down this tunnel."

"The map hasn't lied so far, right?" Kyle asked.

"Right."

"So, now we need to figure out what the map is telling us," Kyle said, "and we'll find the gold, right?"

Kimmie threw her backpack on the ground and sat down on top of it. "I guess."

Kyle sat down next to her. "You must be tired. Let's call it a day," he said. "We can come back tomorrow."

Kimmie didn't budge. "Kyle, you're the map expert. Look at it again," she said, pointing to the map in Kyle's hands. "We must have missed something."

Kyle laid the map on the floor of the cave and got on his hands and knees for a closer look. He moved his finger along the lines on the map that indicated the tunnels. He moved his finger back and forth several times. "Nothing jumps out at me."

Kimmie pointed at the wall opposite where they were sitting. "Too bad that's not a vein of gold. Our treasure hunt would be over," she said.

Kyle looked across the cave where Kimmie was pointing. A quartz vein ran diagonally down the cave wall and disappeared under the cave floor. He got up and walked across the cave. As he got closer, he noticed small flakes of gold encased in the quartz. He followed the vein to the floor. At the point where the floor and the wall intersected, the gold flakes were more concentrated than higher up in the vein.

Kyle jumped up and slapped his hands together. "Kimmie, I know where the gold is."

"Where?" she asked.

"The gold is under this cave floor."

"Under the floor?"

Kyle went back to the map he'd left on the floor. "Yep, under the floor," he said with a grin. "We saw markings on the map that indicated the gold was right in front of us, right?"

"Yes?"

"Well," said Kyle, as he pointed to the marks on the map. "These hash marks indicate that there is something in front of us—sort of. The marks are dashed because they are showing something in the cave but indicating it's beneath the floor. And that something is what I believe is the gold—right in front of us, and below us."

Kimmie scooted closer to Kyle and looked at the map, then looked at the floor in front of them. "Okay," she said, "but I don't see any signs that Gramps did any digging here to get to the gold under the floor."

"That's because he didn't dig here."

"So where did he dig?"

"I think when he saw that quartz vein, he realized he could get to the gold an easier way without having to dig through this floor." Kyle flipped the map around and pointed to an area close to the cabin. "See this mark right here? This is another cave entrance. If you follow the positions of this cave entrance and where we are now, they fit together."

Kimmie leaned even closer to Kyle. "And?"

Kyle hit the map with his finger. "That's where we'll find the gold of Morgan Gulch."

# 17

# CAVE OF GOLD

After a restless night waiting for morning to come, Kyle stood on the porch, once again waiting for Kimmie. He took a long, deep breath. "I just love it up here. It's even better with the smell of gold in the air," he said to himself.

"I know what you mean," said Kimmie bounding out the back door. "But let's not count our gold bars before they've hardened."

"Good one, Kimmie," said Kyle. "Well, sis, are you ready for this? This day will go down in Morgan history as the greatest day ever."

Kyle started down the road to the cabin. "I wished I'd seen that clue on the map before we hiked all the way up to Boca Grande. We were so close to that cave entrance."

"I wish you had too," replied Kimmie. "This hiking stuff is getting to be a pain."

The walk to the cabin was fun. They saw a couple of deer grazing and a fat porcupine waddling his way up the mountain. It was a perfect day for discovering gold.

Once at the cabin, they rested before hiking up to the cave. Sitting on one of the tree stump chairs, Kyle watched the stream. "This is great," he said. "From right here, I can see lots of great fishing holes. We'll have to bring Grandpa up here. I bet there's hundreds of trout."

Kimmie tightened her backpack. "Well, let's finish this fishing trip before we start another one, okay? You're not very good at doing more than one thing at a time."

Kyle sneered. He stood up and looked in the direction of the cave that was north of Boca Grande, but lower in elevation.

Kyle pointed to a large, dark section of the mountain about one hundred yards up the hill from the stream. "There is it, Kimmie," he exclaimed. "The cave of gold."

Kimmie grinned, but had tears in her eyes. "The greatest treasure hunt of all times is just about to end."

"Well," Kyle said, "maybe the greatest, but it's certainly not going to be the last. There's so much history in this valley, The Indians, the miners, the mountain men. We'll be hunting treasure for years."

Kimmie slapped Kyle on the back. "I didn't think you wanted to stick around this ol' place any longer than you had to."

Kyle shrugged. "I didn't give the mountain much of a chance, did I?"

Kimmie snorted. "Are you kidding? None at all."

They started up the steep hill. The closer they got to the entrance, the more Kyle felt Gramps's presence. He knew that inside the cave was the gold Gramps had found and left for his family. He knew Gramps had left the gold for him to find—no one else. Gramps had been gone for a very long time, and there were plenty of chances for other people to find the map, the cave, and the gold. Kyle knew that somehow, Gramps had protected the map and the gold, and kept them safe for him.

Kyle aimed his headlamp into the cave entrance. He leaned forward and saw that the floor to the cave was about ten feet down. Just in the nick of time, he caught Kimmie from falling. He grabbed her shirt and pulled her back.

"What are you doing?" asked Kimmie.

"Saving your life," Kyle said. "Take a peek—slowly."

Kimmie eased herself toward the edge of the cave entrance. "Oh my gosh!" she cried. "How are we going to get down?"

Kyle brushed away the dirt from the lip of the entrance. Attached to the wall was an old rope ladder. Kyle looked down to the bottom of the cave. The ladder hung down to about two feet above the floor. Kyle moved his light around, hoping to get a glimpse of some gold piles. All he saw was a wall, not far from the ladder.

Kyle sat at the edge of the entrance. "I'll go down first," he told Kimmie. "I'll stay at the bottom of the ladder just in case."

"I'll be fine," said Kimmie. "But if it would make you feel better, you can stand by the ladder—just in case."

Kyle knew what she meant. She was afraid of heights. He was to stay at the bottom of the ladder to catch her if she fell.

He turned and stepped carefully onto the ladder. He knew the rope ladder would be worn from years of exposure. The first rung held fine. He stepped to the second one and felt a slight slip of the rope. He gripped it tighter. He stepped down to the next rung, then to the next. One more, then he jumped to the floor.

"Whew. Your turn," he called up to Kimmie. "Be careful. The ladder slipped a little on the second rung."

Kimmie turned around and put her foot on the first rung. "Okay," she said. "Coming down." She took each step cautiously—one, two, three. As she stepped onto the fourth rung, the ladder slipped several inches. "Aaah!"

"Hold on," Kyle said. "There's just one more step then you'll be down."

As Kimmie stepped down onto the last rung, Kyle reached up and helped her to the ground. "I've got you."

"I hope that ladder holds going back up," said Kimmie. "I'm not prepared to live as a hermit in this dark place for a hundred years."

"We'll be fine," Kyle said.

They walked down the damp, narrow corridor. Water dripped from the ceiling, making pools on the ground along the way. The roots that hung down into the cave from the bushes above ground, got caught in their hair. Kimmie shuddered and hung on tightly to Kyle's belt loop.

Based on the markings on the map, Kyle had estimated how far they would need to walk before they reached the spot where the gold should be. Just as he was second-guessing his estimation, they turned a corner, and his light brightened up a large room. Suddenly, he stopped, causing Kimmie to slam into him.

Kimmie didn't let go of Kyle's belt loop. "What's wrong?" She asked, her voice trembling. "Why did you stop?"

"We've come to the end of the tunnel," Kyle said. "Kimmie, look."

Kimmie slowly peeked around Kyle's back. There in front of them was Gramps's gold. Kyle took his headlamp off his head and used it like a hand-held flashlight to get a better view of the room. He moved his light from one corner to the other and back again. The floor of the room was covered in gold. The pile had to be at least six inches deep in some places. Gramps had found the mother lode.

Kimmie shrieked as she jumped up and down. "It's hard to believe there's really gold, Kyle," she said. "Grandpa's rich!"

Kyle hugged Kimmie, then danced a Scottish jig. They both laughed and slapped several high-fives. Kyle knelt down and touched the gold. Kimmie knelt beside him staring with her mouth gaping open. They used their bandanas to wipe away dirt from the gold that had obviously been dug out of the cave wall or out of rocks. There was a pile of gold nuggets that were much cleaner and purer than the rest. Kyle guessed that Gramps had chiseled the gold out of the rock, not wanting to haul the extra weight to the surface.

Kyle picked up several of the nuggets and studied them closely. He picked out one of the larger but manageable nuggets and put it in his backpack. He had to take the proof back to Grandpa.

Kyle stood up, brushing the dirt off his pants. "My headlamp is flickering. We need to get out of here before we lose our light," he said. "I'm sure it's getting late too. We don't want Grandpa to worry."

"Grandpa is going to be so happy," Kimmie said, her voice quivering a bit.

Kyle shined the headlamp toward Kimmie's face. He thought he saw a tear rolling down her cheek.

"Yes, he'll be happy, once he stops yelling at us for staying out past dark if we don't hurry." Kyle took one last look at the gold and jumped and hit the ceiling. "I knew it!"

Kimmie led the way back to the ladder. As they walked, Kyle felt as though someone was following him. He turned around and looked behind him several times. He was certain it was Gramps, but it still felt creepy, especially down in this dark corridor where there was no easy escape.

Kyle had Kimmie climb up the ladder first. "If something happens to the ladder while you're climbing up, I'll be able to catch you," he told her. "If it breaks on my way up, you run and get help. We didn't bring our ropes, so there's no way to get me out without some extra help. Okay?"

"Okay," Kimmie said. "But nothing's going to happen."

"Right," Kyle said. He helped Kimmie get started up the ladder and held her steady for as long as he could. He stood ready to catch her if the ladder broke free from the lip of the entrance. Kyle kept talking to her trying to keep her mind off the climb, doing his best to keep her from being afraid.

Just as Kimmie was starting to pull herself out into the sunlight, she slipped. One side of the ladder broke free, and she started to fall. Kyle held on to the ladder and positioned himself to catch her. All of a sudden, Kimmie stopped falling. She regained her grip on the rope and pulled herself out of the cave.

Kimmie poked her head over the edge. Even from down below, Kyle could tell the slip had scared her badly.

"Are you okay?" Kyle didn't wait for an answer. In his gym class at school in Arizona, the boys used to race each other up a rope, touch the ceiling of the gymnasium, and race back to the floor. He usually won.

He pulled firmly on the secure side of the ladder. The quicker he climbed the ladder, the better chance he had of making it to the top before the other side came loose.

Kyle put his foot on the first rung, took a deep breath, putting one hand over the other, letting his feet dangle so they wouldn't slow him down. Kyle was up the rope and out of the entrance quickly. Kimmie grabbed him and threw her arms around him. "Thank you," she said. "You saved my life."

"What?"

"If you hadn't caught me, I'd probably be dead by now," she said in her usual, melodramatic tone.

"No, I would have caught you at the bottom. I wouldn't have let you get hurt." Kyle was puzzled by her comment. "Do you think I caught you from falling?"

"Well, didn't—" Kimmie's face turned pale.

"No, I didn't catch you. I was still at the bottom of the ladder," Kyle said. "I was trying to get to you when it looked like you caught yourself and pulled yourself up and out."

"N-no," Kimmie said, even more pale than before. "I didn't catch myself. You put your hand on my back and pushed me up and out of the cave."

Kyle and Kimmie both peered over the edge of the cave entrance.

Kimmie turned to Kyle, her face as white as ghost. "Kyle, there was someone else on that ladder with me."

# 18

## FAMILY REUNION

"Slow down. One at a time please," Grandpa said waving his hands in the air. He turned back to the stove and stirred the hot chocolate. "You can tell me all about your adventure over a nice cup of hot chocolate. You both look like you could use two or three."

Grandpa was right. Kyle and Kimmie looked like they had been dragged around the mountain by a runaway horse. They were covered in dirt, head to toe, a few scrapes here and there, and a few new holes in their hiking clothes.

"What's this, Kimmie?" Grandpa asked, brushing her hair away from her face. "You have little flecks of glittering stuff all over your face." Grandpa poured their hot chocolate and topped off each cup with a handful of tiny marshmallows—another one of Kimmie's favorites.

"It's gold, Grandpa," Kimmie said.

Grandpa laughed. "Ghosts and gold. You two have really taken this treasure hunting to the next level, haven't you?"

"That's what we want to talk to you about," said Kyle. "But before we tell you what happened, you have to see this." Kyle reached into his backpack and pulled out the gold nugget.

Grandpa's face went pale. "Wh-where did this come from?"

"Your mountain, Grandpa," Kyle said. "When we found Gramps's old treasure map in the cabin, we figured out where the gold was. There's a lot more in the cave, Grandpa—lots more."

Grandpa's chin quivered. "Thank you, Kyle. Thank you, Kimmie. Thank you so very much."

"Grandpa," Kyle said. "There is enough gold in that cave to cover this kitchen floor and stack it two feet high. You have enough gold to buy lots of ranches."

Grandpa stared at the nugget. It was as large as a baseball. It was made up of almost all gold with very little rock in it. He turned it over and over in his hand. "I'm not sure if you know just how much this means to me—to all of us," Grandpa said. "You have saved my dignity and the family ranch. I can't thank you enough." He gave each of them a hug.

Kyle and Kimmie turned and looked at each other. They raised their hands and slapped a high-five. Kimmie giggled.

"Now," Grandpa said, wiping the tears from his eyes. "Tell me about your adventure."

Kyle and Kimmie took turns telling their story. Of course, as with most stories, there was more drama in the telling than in the adventure, but Grandpa said it was the greatest story he had ever heard.

Kimmie moved from her chair and sat on Grandpa's lap. "There was something very strange that happened while we were climbing out of the tunnel," she said.

"What do you mean, Kimmie?" Grandpa asked. "Could there be anything stranger than what I've already heard?"

"Way stranger," Kimmie said. "As I got to the top of the ladder, just as I was reaching up to grab the lip of the cave entrance, one side of the ladder broke loose from the dirt. I held the rope as tightly as I could, but I kept falling."

Grandpa gave Kimmie a squeeze. "You don't look like you got hurt. What happened next?"

"That's the strange thing, Grandpa," Kimmie said. "I didn't get hurt. Something—no, somebody—stopped me from falling to the ground."

"Well, it had to have been Kyle. He was right there with you."

"No, Kyle was on the ground." Kimmie stood up. With arms flying and legs flailing, she described the scene where she fell down the ladder. "Somebody else caught me and helped me out of the cave."

Before Grandpa could ask the inevitable question, Kyle said. "I know it was Gramps."

"Has your brother been telling you some of his ghost stories?" asked Grandpa.

"A few, Grandpa, but this one is true."

Kyle reached into his backpack again and put the rest of the things from the cabin on the table. "I brought some papers, Gramps's diary, and some other treasures from the cabin," he told Grandpa. "I think we need to show a few of them to Tommy and his parents. They need to know what happened up there."

Grandpa took the diary and slowly turned the pages, absorbing the details of his grandfather's writings. Chin quivering, he shook his head. "How is it that I didn't see the clues from Gramps? How is it that I let this go on for so long? What a waste."

"It's not too late, Grandpa," Kyle said. "Let's go first thing in the morning and show the Dunhams what we've found."

Grandpa nodded. "Now, I think you two should get cleaned up and get to bed. It's late, and you've had quite a day."

By the time he was finally in bed, Kyle was exhausted, but he couldn't sleep. Questions about Gramps were on his mind. How could the ghost of someone who had passed away so many years ago be able to influence what is happening now? How is it a ghost could save someone's life? He knew those were two questions he would never be able to answer.

He looked out the window at the mountain, and he wondered what other secrets it was hiding. Would he ever find out? Or were there secrets that would be revealed to one of his own great-great grandchildren? He knew that he would never stop looking for that next adventure. He wasn't sure how any treasure hunt or adventure could ever be better than this one.

Early the next morning Kyle, Kimmie, and Grandpa stood in Tommy's family room. Tommy scowled at them as they waited for his mother to join them.

"I only have a few minutes," said Mrs. Dunham, as she sat down next to Tommy. "What is it that you need to tell us?"

Kyle sat down next to Mrs. Dunham and told her the details of their adventure. After he was done, he handed her the diary and the letter. Kyle told her about the other things they had found. He described the headstone that Gramps had made for her great-grandpa and how Gramps had buried him next to the river where they loved to fish together after a long day of digging for gold. As she read the note from Gramps to her great-grandpa, she sobbed and held the paper tightly to her chest.

"There's more, Mrs. Dunham," Kyle said. He dug into his backpack and pulled out the big gold nugget he had taken from the cave. "Gramps did find gold. We think that your great-grandpa may have helped him dig it up. We'd like to share it with you. I'm sure Gramps would have done the same if he'd lived long enough."

Kimmie handed Mrs. Dunham the picture she had found in the box. "I want you to have this too, Mrs. Dunham. I think it would nice for you to hang on your wall."

"Kyle, Kimmie," Mrs. Dunham said. "We can't accept these things. We don't have a right to take what isn't ours."

"You're family, Betsy," Grandpa said. "We'd like you to have some of the gold. There is something else we'd like to give back to you. Kyle and Kimmie's adventure rekindled my interest in the forgotten history of the mountain, so I went through some of my father's files." Grandpa handed Mrs. Dunham an envelope.

Tommy's mom opened it and pulled out a crinkled, yellowed document. "What is this, Charles?"

His voice shaking and his chin quivering, Grandpa said, "It's the deed to your papa Morgan's property. It has a mining claim on it. Attached to the deed was a note from your great-grandpa asking my grandpa to pass this along to your family. It appears that even my dad is guilty of fueling this feud by withholding these papers from your family. For that, I am deeply sorry."

Mrs. Dunham put her hand to her mouth and gasped. For the first time since he had met Tommy, Kyle saw a compassionate side of him as he handed his mom a tissue and put his arm around her as she read the deed.

Tommy's mom stood up and hugged Grandpa. The years of anger and distance faded away as they walked arm in arm into the kitchen. Tommy's mom offered Grandpa a cup of hot chocolate—with marshmallows.

# 19

## HOME AT LAST

"I'm mighty proud of you, Kyle," Grandpa said, as they walked home. "What you did was difficult, I know. You have done well for our family. Gramps would be proud of you too."

"Thanks, Grandpa," Kyle said. "But it wasn't as hard as you think. It was the right thing to do, and I was glad to do it. Even if Tommy's family doesn't have the riches that we have found on our property, they deserve to have what is rightfully theirs."

Grandpa chuckled. "You never cease to amaze me, Kyle. Before we know it, you'll be wise beyond your years." Grandpa rubbed Kyle's head, and they finished their walk home, talking about all the plans Kyle had for the summer. Kimmie skipped along in front of them.

"We're off to see the Wizard," she sang.

Kyle stopped walking and looked at his grandpa. "There is something I'd like to do for Tommy's family."

"What's that, my boy?"

Rubbing his chin, Kyle said, "I'd like to buy a new headstone for Tommy's papa Morgan and have what's carved in the stone at his grave, replicated on the new headstone," Kyle said, nodding his head. "Yeah, I think that would be perfect."

"I think you're right, Kyle," said Grandpa. "We'll get started on that right away."

That night, as Kyle was doing his chores in the barn, he leaned against the door and looked up to the mountain. Much to his surprise and despite his earlier reluctance, he had found his place at Morgan Gulch. He would never get tired of the mountain and the mysteries it held deep inside.

Kyle looked forward to summer break when he could walk the mountain again on the way to a new adventure. He hoped he would have plenty of time to discover what this valley was all about. He was proud to be a Morgan, and wanted to do everything he could to make his mark on the valley just as his great-great grandpa had done.

Kyle finished his chores and gave the horses their buckets of oats. He shut the barn doors and started toward the house. Out of the corner of his eye, he saw a man leaning against the fence post. At first, Kyle thought it was Grandpa, but he felt the same presence he had felt in the cabin, and again in the cave where they found the gold. He took a few steps toward the man. It was Gramps. There he stood, dressed in his mining clothes, with a pickax in one hand and his mining hat in the other.

"Thank you, Gramps," Kyle shouted.

Gramps put on his felt hat, lit the candle, and swung the pickax over his shoulder. Smiling, he waved to Kyle and turned toward the mountain. He walked off into the forest whistling an old Scottish tune. Kyle laughed. "That's a Morgan for you."

Kyle stepped up onto the porch and took one last look at Old Baldy before going inside for the night. He smiled as he watched the light move across the side of the mountain just as he had seen before. Kyle nodded and took a deep breath. "Home at last, Kyle Morgan, home at last."

# About the Author

Vickie L. Gardner is an author of children's stories, middle grade fiction novels, and short stories. She has had a passion for writing since she was a young girl. She is a three-time graduate of the Institute of Children's Literature, and a member of the Society of Children's Book Writers and Illustrators, and of the Pikes Peak Writers Group of Colorado. Vickie enjoys music, photography, jewelry making, and spending time with her family. While she is enjoying another favorite hobby, traveling, she is always on the lookout for new ideas for her next story. Vickie grew up in Littleton, Colorado, where she lives with her husband. She has two children and four grandchildren.